Subtitle: First Omens of Ragnarök
Author & Editor: Shreyas Koshti.

Address your inquiries below:

Author
Shreyas Koshti
koshtisv@gmail.com
PCMC, Pune.

First Edition: July 2025.

ISBN Paperback: 978-93-343-5360-0

Printed By: [KDP]
Cover by: Self
Published by: Shreyas Koshti. (Self-Published-KDP)

Disclaimer

This book is a work of fiction. Names, characters, places, events, and incidents are either the products of the author's imagination or are used in a fictitious manner for storytelling purposes. The inclusion of real-world figures such as Baba Vanga is purely fictional and intended to enhance the narrative. No claim is made to accurately represent the real beliefs, actions, or prophecies of Baba Vanga or any other historical or public figures referenced.

The author does not intend to offend, defame, or misrepresent any individual, group, or culture. All interpretations and portrayals are fictionalized for entertainment purposes and should not be taken as factual or representative of real-world truths.

Readers are encouraged to treat this book as a creative work and not as a source of historical or biographical accuracy.

"In the heart of a city that never sleeps, where shadows whisper secrets and the air crackles with untold mysteries, a single blue light flickered, heralding the beginning of an end that no one saw coming."

SHAKHTI

"First Omens of Ragnarök"

By

SHREYAS KOSHTI

To my sister, whose unwavering support and love have been my guiding light.

And to my beloved friends, who have stood by me through every twist and turn of this journey.

Thank you for believing in me.

CONTENTS

Acknowledgments

Writing this novel has been an incredible journey, and I am deeply grateful to everyone who has supported me along the way.

First and foremost, I would like to thank my family for their unwavering support and encouragement. Your belief in me has been my greatest motivation.

To my friends and colleagues, thank you for your patience and understanding during the countless hours I spent immersed in writing. Your feedback and insights have been invaluable.

A special thanks to my writing group, whose constructive criticism and camaraderie have helped shape this story into what it is today. Your passion for storytelling is truly inspiring.

I am also grateful to my editor, whose keen eye and thoughtful suggestions have greatly improved this manuscript. Your dedication and expertise have been instrumental in bringing this novel to life.

To the readers, thank you for embarking on this journey with me. Your enthusiasm and support mean the world to me, and I hope this story resonates with you as much as it has with me.

Lastly, I would like to acknowledge the countless authors and storytellers who have inspired me over the years. Your works have ignited my imagination and fueled my passion for writing.

Thank you all for being a part of this adventure.

"Everything started with mysterious murders, sudden surge in crimes in the city, followed by the presence of supernatural entities. Let's begin this journey towards the end of world."

"Amar hurried through the sterile corridors of the forensic department, the echo of his footsteps bouncing off the cold, tiled walls. His mind was a whirlwind of thoughts, each more troubling than the last. As he approached the post-mortem cell, the familiar scent of antiseptic mixed with the faint, lingering odor of death hit him, bringing him back to the grim reality of his work."

CHAPTER

ONE MYSTERIOUS MURDERS

Amar Yadav had been stationed at the Andheri police station for the past year, a placement that marked the beginning of a significant chapter in his career. Despite his young age—just 26 or 27 years old—Amar had made a name for himself, known for cracking complex cases and helping bring justice to many. His youthful appearance often surprised those who knew of his reputation, but beneath that exterior was a sharp, determined mind that had quickly risen through the tough times.

The group of accused criminals who found themselves entangled in Amar's investigations had been left in a state of shock. They hadn't anticipated such a relentless pursuit from someone so young. Amar's success didn't go unnoticed; even Pravin Jagtap, the seasoned Mumbai Police Commissioner, took note of his work. Jagtap had invited Amar to his home, a rare occurrence that underscored the gravity of the situation.

The atmosphere in the commissioner's sturdy was palpably tense. Jagtap, a man in his early 60s, was a hardened veteran of the force, with a wealth of experience dealing with the city's criminal underworld. He was known for his unorthodox methods, often delivering justice on the streets before the courts could intervene. As Amar entered the room, he felt a slight unease, heightened by the imposing presence of the ex-commissioner.

Jagtap sat across from him, polishing his glasses in his hand, a gesture that seemed almost casual but carried an underlying tension. He wore his glasses and with the uneasy feeling he settled on his chair. He appeared uncomforted by the open rubber lining on his frame. Removing his glasses, Jagtap leaned forward, his sharp eyes narrowing as he scrutinized Amar. Despite his age, Jagtap's reputation as a fearsome enforcer had not waned. His hands, weathered from years of service, trembled slightly as he put down the glass—a subtle sign of the pressure he was under. Jagtapji noticed the concerned face of Amar and quickly reminded of his financial favor on Amar in the days of pandemic.

"Don't worry if you need more time, Amar," Jagtap began, his voice heavy with authority. "If it's my money on the line, I'm not concerned."

Amar, always respectful, replied, "No, sir, I have started feeling guilty about it. I remember how you have helped me through the rough patch of my life. Now, I've learned to handle these situations. I owe a lot to the force and especially you—it's like my second family." He paused; his curiosity piqued.

"But why did you call me here today, sir?"

Jagtap's gaze hardened. "I was in Pune recently," he explained. "I met an officer much like you—sharp, driven. There's a case involving Mansukh Khan and Javed Ustad. I'm transferring it to your station through my active sources. While Mansukh Khan isn't my concern anymore, Javed Ustad's movements have been troubling. I suspect he's planning something big. I want you to set up an indirect encounter of him. I have several evidences which might be very useful for framing a case against him and we will divert the attention to his enemies. Jay needs a reliable support to execute this assignment."

Jagtap's words carried the weight of his experience. As the ex-commissioner of Mumbai, he had seen the city's darkest corners, especially the crimes orchestrated by those with ties to Dubai as well as the Islamic State. His approach to law enforcement was ruthless; he believed in swift justice, often bypassing the legal system to ensure criminals were dealt with before they could escape the law's reach.

He had trained his officers to operate under the radar, to handle situations that required more than just a badge. These officers would ensure that justice was served, often by eliminating the threat entirely. Jay, one of Jagtap's most trusted men, had been executing these covert operations since he was just eighteen, staging events to look like natural causes or accidents, leaving no trace of police involvement. Jay was uplifted through several trainings while he was studying and was serving as an undercover agent in IB. Jay has a record of some cross border missions and had an extraordinary skill of blending into the surrounding. He had a major contribution in several diplomatic movements and gathering support information before carrying out a surgical strike. These agents directly and indirectly protecting country in either way. Nobody was aware of people like Jay were involved in covert operations as it was personally taken care by the chief security officers. Jagtap was directly commanded by them.

The criminals of Mumbai feared these shadowy figures, knowing that their reach extended far beyond that of the government. They knew that once targeted by Jagtap's team, their days were numbered. Decisions were made on the spot, and justice was served swiftly, without the delays of a courtroom trial.

Amar fell in deep thoughts as he started planning for what is coming in future. He quickly grasped a pen and started writing some dates on the paper. Jagtap looking at him keenly to connect dots and understand what is he planning. Before Amar even completes his plan, he got the call- there was a murder report by a constable.

"Sir, I need to leave. I will update you with the plan and pass instructions for Jay", Amar said and left.

In a rush, Amar reaches the crime scene. He asked the constable who had secured the scene.

"Where was the body found?"

The constable, Patil, exchanged a glance with Nikam, who then motioned for Amar to follow him.

Nikam led Amar down a narrow, unpaved path. After about five minutes of walking, they came upon a gruesome sight—a body lying in the bushes with a face so disfigured it was barely recognizable. As Amar stepped closer, he noticed a gold necklace on the corpse's left hand, which was splayed out on the ground. The right hand was folded unnaturally, and the legs were bent awkwardly. The victim was dressed in only a half-sleeved shirt, and the body was leaning to the right, emitting a foul odor that indicated it had been decomposing for a few days.

"Looks like it's been here for two or three days," Amar said, assessing the scene. "Check for any possessions. Patil, go get the biometric scanner from your car. See if we can identify the body."

Amar took a few steps back from the crime scene, sliding his hand inside the pocket. He retrieved a packet of cigarettes and lit one with the lighter from his upper pocket. Patil quickly returned with the biometric scanner, and after few moments, they had an ID. Patil showed the screen to Amar.

"It's Kamlesh," Patil said, recognizing the name. "We received a missing person's report on him a few days ago. I have confirmed with station records. I'll send the body for a post-mortem examination."

"Good," Amar replied, taking a final drag from his cigarette before dropping it to the ground, he shouted, "Search the surrounding area. Let's see if we can find any more clues."

The area was dense with trees, part of the grounds of the Maruti Temple, which was surrounded by forest. This stretch of road, bordering the national highway, was desolate—known for wild animals and rarely traveled by anyone. As Nikam scanned the area, his eyes caught a blood-stained stone and a bag lying nearby. He carefully picked up the bag and found a passport inside. Flipping it open, he discovered it belonging to a woman named Sharda Suryavanshi.

Amar, now more alert, quickly dialed a number on his mobile phone. "Hello, I'm sending you a photo of a passport. Track down any contact details you can find for this woman and get back to me as soon as possible."

Within a short time, an ambulance arrived at the scene and the body was promptly sent to the lab for further examination. Amar instructed Nikam to accompany him, while he directed Patil to go along with the ambulance and handle the necessary post-mortem protocols.

As they reached the open road and Amar was about to get into the car, a strange sensation washed over him—he felt as though someone was watching him. The day was drawing to a close and the evening shadows were lengthening. Dismissing the feeling as a trick of the fading light, Amar shook it off, got into the car, and made his way back to the station.

Upon arriving at the station, Amar made his way to the desk where Bodke, the computer operator, was intently focused on his work. Without wasting any time, Amar asked, "Bokya, did you manage to find out anything about that woman? And have you informed the deceased's family?"

At the station, everyone affectionately referred to Bodke as 'Bokya.' He was young officer who had previously served in the Cyber Crime Division and now specially sent to work with Amar by Jagtap. He was living with his uncle in Mumbai. Known for his sharp mind and keen investigative skills, Bokya was the go-to person for anything related to digital traces and background checks.

Bodke looked up from his computer screen as Amar approached, his eyes sharp behind his glasses. He adjusted his chair slightly and cracked his knuckles before responding.

"Amar, I've dug up some interesting details," Bodke said, his voice carrying a hint of curiosity. "The woman you're asking about—her name is Sharda Suryavanshi aka Radhika. She's not exactly who she appears to be."

Amar leaned closer, his eyes narrowing. "What do you mean?"

"Well, she's been using multiple aliases," Bodke continued, his fingers flying across the keyboard as he pulled up more files. "But the most consistent identity links her to a series of small-time cons. She's careful, though, never anything too big—just enough to stay under the radar. But what's strange is that she's been quiet for the past year or so. No activity, no new aliases, nothing."

Amar's brow furrowed as he processed the information. "So, what brought her back into the spotlight?"

"That's the thing," Bodke said, his tone growing more serious. "She's connected to a couple of people who've been under investigation recently—one of them, a known associate in a human trafficking ring. It's possible she was laying low until something—or someone—drew her out."

Amar nodded, his mind racing through the possibilities. "And what about the deceased's family? Have they been informed?"

Bodke sighed, shaking his head. "Not yet. I was waiting to confirm a few more details before making the call. Didn't want to give them incomplete information."

"Good call," Amar said. "But we'll need to inform them soon. This case is getting more complicated by the minute."

As if on cue, Amar's phone buzzed in his pocket. He pulled it out and glanced at the screen, his expression darkening as he read the message.

"Damn," he muttered under his breath.

"What is it?" Bodke asked, noticing the change in Amar's demeanor.

"It's a message from PM cell" Amar replied, already turning towards the door. "They've found something unusual—the organs in the body are fused together. I need to head over there now."

Bodke's eyes widened slightly, but he gave a curt nod. "I'll continue digging on this woman."

"Will do," Amar said, already moving out of the station. His mind was racing with thoughts of what he might find at the forensic office. This case was taking a darker turn and he had a feeling that whatever was waiting for him in that post-mortem room was going to be crucial.

As he left the station, Amar couldn't shake the feeling that they were just scratching the surface of something much bigger—and far more dangerous.

Amar hurried through the sterile corridors of the forensic department, the echo of his footsteps bouncing off the cold, tiled walls. His mind was a whirlwind of thoughts, each more troubling than the last. As he approached the post-mortem cell, the familiar scent of antiseptic mixed with the faint, lingering odor of death hit him, bringing him back to the grim reality of his work.

He pushed open the heavy door to find Dr. Arjun, the forensic pathologist, already standing beside the autopsy table. The room was dimly lit, with only the overhead surgical light illuminating the body laid out on the stainless-steel table. Dr. Arjun, clad in his white lab coat, looked up as Amar entered, his expression a mixture of concern and fascination.

"Amar, you need to see this." Dr. Arjun said, his voice steady but laced with unease. He gestured towards the body on the table, a middle-aged woman, her skin pale and waxy under the harsh light.

Amar stepped closer, his gaze fixed on the man's abdomen, which had been carefully opened by Dr. Arjun. What he saw made his stomach churn—a mass of organs, fused together in a way that defied all logic. The liver melded into the stomach, which in turn was indistinguishable from the intestines. It was as if her internal organs had melted and congealed into one grotesque lump of tissue.

"This… this isn't natural," Amar murmured, his eyes widening in disbelief. "What could have caused something like this?"

Dr. Arjun shook his head, his face grim. "I've never seen anything like it. At first, I thought it might be some kind of severe congenital disorder, but even that doesn't explain this level of fusion. The tissues are completely interwoven—there's no clear distinction between them."

Amar reached out, almost hesitant, as if touching the body would somehow make the horror of it more real. "Any signs of external trauma? Poisoning?"

"No external trauma that would cause this," Dr. Arjun replied, folding his arms across his chest. "And the toxicology report is still pending, but I doubt it's a simple case of poisoning. This is something… different."

As Amar absorbed the gravity of Dr. Arjun's words, his gaze wandered across the room, taking in the details almost unconsciously. That's when he noticed a pair of surgical blades on the floor near the autopsy table. They were fused together at the edges, as if they had melted into each other. He frowned slightly, puzzled by the sight, but his mind quickly dismissed it as some oddity of the room, a malfunction with the sterilization equipment perhaps. There were more pressing concerns at hand, and he pushed the thought aside.

Before Amar could respond to Dr. Arjun, his phone buzzed again, the sound unnervingly loud in the quiet room. He pulled it out, the ominous feeling from earlier deepening as he saw the caller ID. It was from the station.

He answered, pressing the phone to his ear. "Amar here."

The voice on the other end was urgent, almost frantic. "Sir, we've just received a report of another body. Same condition—hands fused together. This time it's a young man, found in a different part of the area."

Amar's grip tightened on the phone, his jaw clenching as the implications sank in. "I'll be there right away," he said, ending the call and slipping the phone back into his pocket.

He turned to Dr. Arjun; his expression steely. "We've got another one. Same condition."

Dr. Arjun's eyes widened, but he nodded, understanding the gravity of the situation. "Amar, this isn't a coincidence. Someone—or something—is doing this."

Amar nodded, his mind already shifting gears. "We need to find out what connects these victims, and fast. I'll head to the scene. Keep me updated on anything else you find here."

With a final glance at the grotesque scene before him, and ignoring the unsettling sight of the fused surgical blades now fading from his thoughts, Amar turned and strode out of the post-mortem cell, his mind racing with the implications of what he had just seen. The mystery was deepening, and the clock was ticking.

Amar arrived at the scene, his mind still racing from the bizarre discovery at the post-mortem room. He quickly advanced toward the dead body, his sharp eyes scanning the surroundings. Nikam was already there, crouched beside the lifeless figure, meticulously examining the area. As Amar approached, Nikam stood up, wiping his hands on a cloth.

"I've identified the body," Nikam said, his voice steady despite the grim circumstances. "It's Vikram Joshi, a local—mid-thirties, no significant criminal record, but connected to a few shady characters. Found with the same bizarre condition. Just like the others."

Amar nodded, taking in the details as he leaned in closer to inspect the scene himself. But as he focused on the body, an unsettling feeling washed over him—a sensation of being watched. His instincts flared, and his eyes flicked up, scanning the perimeter. Then he caught a glimpse of movement in the shadows behind the bushes, just beyond the edge of the police cordon.

Someone was there, observing them.

Without hesitation, Amar straightened up, his heart pounding as adrenaline surged through his veins. "Nikam, stay with the scene," he ordered, already moving towards the bushes.

He moved quickly, his footsteps quiet but purposeful, as he approached the spot where he had seen the figure. But as soon as he got close, the man bolted, darting out from the cover of the bushes and sprinting down a narrow alley.

"Hey! Stop!" Amar shouted, giving chase without a second thought. The man was fast, slipping through the tight spaces and winding alleys like a ghost, but Amar was relentless, his breath steady as he closed the gap.

The man glanced over his shoulder, panic flashing in his eyes as he realized Amar was gaining on him. He pushed himself harder, weaving through the alleys until he burst out onto a busy street. There, a car was parked haphazardly at the curb—a getaway vehicle.

The man didn't hesitate. He yanked open the door, jumped inside, and slammed it shut. The engine roared to life as Amar reached the street, and the car peeled away, tires screeching on the asphalt.

Amar didn't miss a beat. He spotted a police jeep parked nearby, one of his men already inside. "Get in!" he shouted, jumping into the passenger seat.

The officer floored the gas, and the jeep lurched forward, the engine growling as they sped after the fleeing car. The chase was on.

They tore through the city streets, weaving between cars and pedestrians, the siren wailing as they pushed the jeep to its limits. The suspect's car swerved dangerously, barely avoiding collisions as it careened around corners, trying to shake off the pursuit. But

Amar's driver was skilled, matching every move, closing the distance with each turn.

As they sped through the crowded market district, the suspect's car clipped a vendor's cart, sending fruits and debris flying into the street. The jeep swerved around the mess, but Amar kept his focus on the car ahead, his mind racing to anticipate the suspect's next move.

Suddenly, from behind, another car appeared, joining the chase. It wasn't police—it was an unmarked vehicle, sleek and black, clearly pursuing the same target. Amar's pulse quickened as he realized they weren't the only ones after the suspect. The black car weaved through traffic with alarming precision, staying close on the suspect's tail.

The chase led them out of the market and onto a deserted stretch of road. The suspect saw his chance and floored the accelerator, the car surging forward with a burst of speed. But Amar wasn't about to let him get away.

"Keep on him!" Amar shouted, his eyes locked on the car ahead. They sped down the road, the gap between them closing as the jeep pushed harder, the engine roaring in pursuit.

Suddenly, the suspect made a sharp turn onto a narrow side street, trying to lose them in the maze of back alleys. Both the police jeep and the black car followed, tires screeching as they took the corner at breakneck speed. The alley was too tight for the suspect's car to maneuver easily, and for a moment, it seemed like they might catch him.

But then, something inexplicable happened. As the suspect's car hurtled down the alley, it seemed to blur for a split second before passing through what appeared to be an invisible wall—a shimmering, glass-like barrier that appeared out of nowhere. The suspect's car vanished through it without a trace.

Amar's eyes widened in disbelief as the black car, following closely, smashed into the invisible barrier with a loud, sickening crunch. The car crumpled upon impact, the front end collapsing like an accordion, but the glass-like wall didn't shatter or crack—it simply shimmered, like a mirage.

The police jeep skidded to a halt just in time, avoiding a collision. Amar and his driver stared in shock at the scene before them. The black car was totaled; its driver slumped over the wheel but miraculously unharmed. The barrier, however, had vanished as quickly as it appeared, leaving nothing but confusion and unanswered questions in its wake.

"What the hell was that?" Amar muttered, still trying to process what he had just witnessed. He jumped out of the jeep, rushing over to the wrecked car. The driver inside was dazed but alive, mumbling incoherently about something he couldn't explain.

Amar's mind raced. The suspect had vanished, escaping through something beyond comprehension. And now, with this mysterious barrier and another party clearly involved, the case had taken a turn into the unknown.

But Amar knew one thing for sure—whatever this was, it was bigger and more dangerous than anything he had faced before. And he was determined to get to the bottom of it, no matter where the chase led him next.

•••

"After walking for approximately half an hour, Amar spotted a faint blue glow advancing slowly through the forest. The glow was circular in shape, and everything that penetrated the strange blue circle fell to the ground, cut by the intense heat it emitted. Branches that had already been cut and were still in contact with the wall glowed with an orange light, indicating a flameless burning."

CHAPTER **TWO** THE FIRST DEMON

Amar approached the car that had wrecked in front of them. A tall man with broad shoulders, clad in a brown leather jacket, stepped out. His head was covered with short hair and a long black beard cascaded down his neck. Amar immediately recognized him as Jay, who had been working for Jagtapji since he was seventeen.

"Too slow, wasn't it?"

Amar remarked with a hint of sarcasm.

Jay smirked, slamming the car door shut as he walked over to Amar.

"Why don't you hand me your car?" Jay suggested, his tone carrying a mix of jest and seriousness.

"Not mine, but I will arrange one for you", Amar replied.

Together, Jay and Amar made their way to the spot where the car had mysteriously vanished. They discovered traces of molten tar on the road, as if a scorching hot, invisible wall had sliced through the asphalt. The sight was both perplexing and alarming, hinting at the strange and dangerous forces at play.

"This is strange! I've never seen anything like this," Jay exclaimed, grabbing a stick from the side of the road.

He cautiously poked it into the invisible wall, only to watch in astonishment as the wooden stick dissolved into particles that floated upwards.

"I think this might be some kind of radioactive shield that instantly evaporates anything that tries to pass through," Amar speculated.

"I think no, Otherwise I would have been in ashes", Jay said.

The two of them began to explore the area, searching for clues about the mysterious phenomenon. Suddenly, they noticed a teenager speeding towards the wall on his bike, helmet on, oblivious to Nikam's frantic shouts and attempts to warn him.

As the bike approached the wall, everyone held their breath in panic. To their shock, the boy passed through the thin wall unscathed.

"Wait, what? He just passed through!" Jay exclaimed, running towards the road. He saw the molten tar retreating into an inch-wide crack left by the invisible wall.

"It's gone," he said in disbelief.

Amar bent down and picked up two stones fused together, just like he had seen before. Jay walks near Amar and looked at the stone.

"Strange! It's something very unnatural." Jay said.

Amar gathered a few more fused stones before they drove to the police station. Upon arrival, they found Jagtapji already waiting for Jay. He was there to hand some of important documents to Jay.

Javed Malik, known as Javed Ustad, had been involved with the underworld for over 15 years. Seven years ago, he was arrested for carrying automatic weapons and using them in public to instill fear among civilians. Before his first arrest, he was deeply involved in drug trafficking, which caught the attention of the underworld. His connections made him powerful enough to commit murders, dispose of bodies, and bribe judges for his release, as if it were a game. Jagtapji wanted him eliminated discreetly, ensuring no police involvement would alert the underworld.

Jay entered the police station, walked up to Jagtapji and bent down to touch his feet, his eyes brimming with emotion.

"I thought I would never see you again after the last incident. I almost got caught." Jay confessed.

"No, son! I would have saved one of my bests." Jagtapji reassured him. He opened his side bag, took out a file, and handed it to Jay. Then, he walked into the sub-inspector's cabin and retrieved a dictionary from the shelf.

"Study the file and keep this dictionary. You will need it," Jagtapji instructed. "By the way, did you meet Kritika?"

Kritika was Jay's childhood friend and confidante. She was a brilliant forensic scientist as well as a psychiatrist with a sharp mind and an unwavering sense of justice. Her dedication to her work often put her at odds with the dangerous world Jay operated in. Despite their different paths, they shared a deep bond, and her insights had often helped Jay in his missions. However, their relationship had become strained due to the risks Jay took and the secrets he kept.

"Nope! We probably won't see each other now," Jay replied, his voice tinged with regret.

"Fine," Jagtapji said, patting Jay's shoulder before leaving.

Amar approached Jay, glanced at the file in his hand, and then picked up the three-inch-thick dictionary, placing it inside a bag on the desk nearby. He handed the bag to Jay.

"Go home! You need rest," Amar advised.

"I feel sorry about what happened with you and Kritika. I just wish everything goes well soon. She will definitely understand one day what you have done for this country."

"I hope so," Jay sighed, taking the bag from Amar and leaving.

"Everybody, back to work," Amar ordered, as the station returned to its usual bustle.

After long five years, Jay finally arrived at his four-room house in Mumbai. He parked his car which Amar arranged for him and walked up to the main door. Jay's house had been constructed by one of bests architects in Mumbai, who had incorporated numerous clever features to make it easy to deceive any intruders. Jay inserted his keys into the lock and turned them, unlocking the door. With his right hand, he pressed a wooden wheel engraved on the door and turned it clockwise. He then grabbed the handle and pushed the door open, stepping inside.

A strong, pungent odor hit him immediately, causing him to pull out his handkerchief and cover his nose. He quickly opened a window and adjusted the curtain to let in some fresh air. The hall was covered in a large cloth, a precaution taken when Jay and Kritika had left the house earlier. Jay pulled the cloth off the sofa and placed his bag on it.

"I need to clean this up," he muttered to himself.

After a tiring day of cleaning, Jay stepped out into the rear passage of his home in the evening. The rear area was spacious enough to accommodate three cars. Beneath the tiles lay a large water tank supplying water to the small garden with an automated system. Jay unlocked the lid of the water tank and jumped inside. Struggling in the dark, water-filled tank, he found a metal railing underwater and followed it to a secret room, emerging on the other side of his home. The house had a hall on the ground floor, two rooms above it, and a hidden section accessible only through the water tank. This ingenious design was perfect for secret activities, and no one could have imagined it.

Jay followed a dim light on the wall and switched on the power supply of the room. The room featured belly-level tables along all the walls, with seven monitors on the north wall displaying real-time camera views of his house and all the roads leading to it. In the center of the room was a square table with a large spotlight hanging over it. Jay quickly opened a sealed wardrobe and tool his laptop out. The room was clean due it being completely isolated from outside atmosphere. There was a small filtered vent provided with force ventilation. Jay had access to the satellite connection specially allotted by

Central. As he switched on the laptop, he received a message from Jagtapji,

"7.45, 24-1, Hotel Green Palace."

Satisfied with his message, Jay leaned back in his chair, reflecting on the day's events. The house, with its hidden secrets and clever design, felt both familiar and strange after so many years. The memories of Kritika and their time together in this house flooded back, mingling with the present reality of his solitary mission. Jay knew that the path ahead was fraught with danger, but he was determined to see it through, no matter the cost.

#

On the same day, Amar decided to return to the location where they had encountered the strange wall. He rode his bike to the edge of the jungle, parked it on the side of the road, and ventured into the dense foliage with a torch in hand. After walking for a minute, he noticed several trees with their branches cut in unnaturally straight lines.

'This is so strange. The wall doesn't seem to have disappeared but moved. The moment it moved, this must have happened,' Amar thought to himself.

He picked up a piece of wood that had been cut by the mysterious wall and collected some ash from one of the burned ends into an evidence bag. Determined to uncover more, he continued deeper into the jungle.

After walking for approximately half an hour, Amar spotted a faint blue glow advancing slowly through the forest. The glow was circular in shape, and everything that penetrated the strange blue circle fell to the ground, cut by the intense heat it emitted. Branches that had already been cut and were still in contact with the wall glowed with an orange light, indicating a flameless burning.

'Here it is. I should keep a safe distance from this thing. It's probably radioactive. If this continues moving forward, it will reach the city by morning!' Amar thought, alarmed.

He quickly took out his phone and began recording the scene. Suddenly, he heard a noise from the bushes. Frightened, Amar stumbled, dropping his phone, and grabbed the torch that had slipped into his rear pocket. He searched the area, sweating and on high alert.

"Who's there? Come out!" Amar shouted, his voice trembling with fear.

He looked around for his phone to call for help but couldn't find it. Panic set in, and he started running towards the highway. Suddenly, he stopped dead in his tracks when he heard the throaty growl of a Leopard emerging from the bushes to his right.

Amar stood still, his heart pounding. He threw his torch away in a desperate attempt to distract the beast, but it didn't work. Seeing no other option, Amar started running again, the leopard roaring and chasing after him. Amar lost his balance and fell to the ground. He quickly turned around and saw the beast leaping towards him, ready to attack.

"Noooooooo!" Amar screamed in terror, covering his face with his hands in a futile attempt to protect himself.

Just as the leopard was about to sink its teeth into him, Amar felt a splash of blood. The leopard's head fell beside him, cleanly severed.

Amar stood up, trying to comprehend what had just happened. He saw three small disks glowing blue, flying around him. The disks descended to the ground, converging towards a tall figure standing in the distance. The dark outline of a man deep in the woods began to grow larger, and with a few steps, the pale moonlight revealed his face.

"You?" Amar asked in surprise, recognizing the man.

...

(News anchor speaking): "...After the man felt comfortable, he gave his statement to the police, implicating Javed in the killings around the city. This is yet to be confirmed by the police department, but dragging a reputed businessman into this could be an attempt to tarnish his image. Now, over to Priya for today's weather report..."

CHAPTER 3

THREE RESURRECTIONS

A shadow emerged from the trees, revealing itself as Dr. Arjun. He had saved Amar from the leopard attack. As he walked closer, he glanced at the pieces of the big cat scattered around them. Amar exhaled in relief, trying to process the harrowing experience. Arjun gave him a moment to collect himself before breaking the silence.

"What are you doing here?" Arjun asked, his voice calm but firm.

"Me? I should be asking you the same question. So, it was you who disappeared this morning with your car on the highway," Amar replied, still shaken.

"Yes, I did. Because I was afraid," Arjun admitted.

"Who are you really?" Amar demanded, his curiosity and frustration mounting.

Arjun, who had demonstrated so many supernatural abilities, knew he owed Amar an explanation. "I don't know how to explain all this right now. Just remember not to disclose this to anyone, and I promise I will explain everything. I am running from the supreme demon among us."

"Supreme demon? Who?" Amar asked, bewildered.

"Can you stop asking so many questions at once? We have to leave this jungle now. He can sense us anywhere. Follow me if you want to live," Arjun instructed, urgency in his voice.

Amar giving final glances to the burning tires and it appeared that all traces were vanished.

Arjun led Amar out of the jungle to his car. Amar hesitated, worried about his bike parked somewhere else on the highway.

"I have my bike parked on the road," he said.

"Don't worry about it," Arjun reassured him.

They both got into the car, and Arjun drove Amar home. As they reached Amar's home, he noticed that the bike was parked there. Amar looked at Arjun with eyes with mixed feelings.

The events of the day weighed heavily on Amar's mind.

"Who is he? I can't get over what happened to me today," he thought as he went to his room. After a long shower to wash off the blood, he fell into a deep sleep.

The next morning, Amar woke up to find Arjun sitting in his room, keenly observing him. Startled, Amar jumped out of bed.

"Surprise! I didn't want to ruin your morning like this, but I wanted to surrender," Arjun said, his tone serious.

"Surrender? I feel like you're making fun of us all by surrendering with all those superpowers you have," Amar retorted, still trying to grasp the situation.

"Nope, not at all. I just want to share everything with you, in detail. Arrest me. I want to keep him distracted," Arjun explained.

"Him Who?", Arjun asked.

"Time will answer everything, I need your help for now so do as I say", Arjun replied.

Amar decided to take Arjun to the abandoned facility where Mr. Jagtap used to train his undercover executors. The building had been under construction but was deemed illegal a few months after it began. Jagtap had taken over the case and secretly built a chamber underneath the building for secret interrogations of ministers, corrupt officers, and other deadly criminals. Before they arrived, Bodake made all the necessary arrangements at the facility as priorly informed by Amar.

As they drove to the facility, Amar couldn't shake the feeling of unease. The roads were eerily quiet, and the tension in the car was palpable. Arjun remained silent; his eyes fixed on the road ahead. Amar's mind raced with questions, but he knew better than to ask them now.

When they arrived at the facility, the atmosphere was thick with anticipation. Bodake greeted them at the entrance, his face stern.

"Everything is ready," he said, leading them to the underground chamber.

The chamber was dimly lit, with a single spotlight illuminating the center of the room. The walls were lined with various interrogation tools, and a large table stood in the middle. Arjun walked to the table and placed his hands on it, looking at Amar.

"This is where it all began," Arjun said, his voice echoing in the chamber. "I need to tell you everything, but first, we need to ensure we are safe."

Suddenly, the lights flickered, and a cold breeze swept through the room. Amar's heart pounded as he looked around, trying to find the source of the disturbance. Arjun's eyes narrowed, and he turned to Amar.

"He's here," Arjun whispered. "The supreme demon has found us."

The room plunged into darkness, and a chilling laugh echoed through the chamber. Amar felt a cold hand on his shoulder and spun around, but there was no one there. Panic set in as the temperature dropped, and the air grew thick with malevolence.

"Stay close to me," Arjun commanded, his voice steady despite the chaos. "We need to fight him off."

Amar nodded, his fear giving way to determination. He had to trust Arjun, no matter how strange the situation was. Together, they faced the darkness, ready to confront the supreme demon and uncover the truth behind the supernatural events that had turned their lives upside down. Suddenly, it felt like everything settled to the calm back again.

After the intense encounter, Amar knew he had to attend the press conference that Jagtapji had mentioned. He turned to Arjun, who was still on high alert.

"I need to go to the press conference. It's crucial for our plan," Amar said, his voice filled with urgency.

"I understand," Arjun replied. "Lock me up in a secure place."

Amar nodded and led Arjun to a hidden room in the basement. The room was fortified with thick walls and a heavy metal door, designed to keep anyone inside safe from external threats. Arjun stepped inside, and Amar locked the door securely.

"I'll be back as soon as I can. Stay safe," Amar said through the small window in the door.

"You too. Be careful," Arjun replied, his eyes filled with concern.

Amar hurried out of the facility, his mind racing with thoughts of the upcoming conference and the dangers that still lurked. He got into his car and drove to the location Jagtapji had sent him.

Upon arriving at the conference venue, Amar saw a crowd of reporters and police officers gathered. He spotted Jagtapji near the entrance and made his way over.

"Amar, glad you could make it," Jagtapji greeted him. "We need to address the public and calm their fears. Are you ready?"

"Yes, I'm ready," Amar replied, taking a deep breath. "Let's do this."

As they walked into the conference room, Amar couldn't help but think about Arjun locked up in his basement. He knew that the battle against the supreme demon was far from over, but for now, he had to focus on the task at hand. The truth would come out, and they would be ready to face whatever came next.

#

Jay was oversleeping in his room when the phone rang. Groggily, he reached for the phone with half-open eyes.

"Hello! Who's this?" he mumbled.

"Jagtap here. The chemicals you requested are ready. A guy will drop them off at the main gate at 10:30. I hope you're prepared for the plan," a deep voice responded.

"Yes, I'm ready. I've made some changes to your plan, but I assure you, Javed will be celebrating his birthday in hell," Jay replied confidently.

"Good," Jagtap said before abruptly ending the call.

Jagtap had devised a plan to execute Javed Ustad on his birthday. After many years, Javed was finally going to be in Mumbai for his grand birthday party.

Jay got out of bed and switched on the TV, tuning into a news channel. He caught part of a news report about Javed Ustad.

(News anchor speaking): "…After the man felt comfortable, he gave his statement to the police, implicating Javed in the killings around the city. This is yet to be confirmed by the police department, but dragging a reputed businessman into this could be an attempt to tarnish his image. Now, over to Priya for today's weather report…"

"Shit! Shit! Shit! This stunt against Javed might cancel his plans to come to Mumbai. I can't let this happen," Jay muttered in frustration.

He quickly called Jagtapji. "We're in trouble. Switch on the TV," Jay urged.

"I saw the headlines. I know what you're thinking. Just calm down. Amar has good news for you. There's a press conference in a moment. Meet me here," Jagtapji replied before cutting the call.

Jay put his phone on charge and started getting ready for the conference. Moments later, an alarm buzzed.

"Probably the guy with the chemicals," Jay thought.

He walked to the main door and found a box with a note on it: "May GOD bless you!"

Jay carried the box inside, opened it, and examined the bottles of chemicals, reading the labels carefully. He placed some of the bottles in the deep freezer. His phone beeped.

"Okay! Time for the good news," Jay said to himself.

He received a text from Jagtapji with the location of venue and left for the conference, ready to face whatever came next.

#

(Distant voice of the present police commissioner on the mic)

"I welcome you all. First of all, I apologize for the short notice of this conference, but given the way news is spreading in the city, we found it very important to address you. I believe that together, the police and the media can prevent people from panicking due to the serial killings that have taken place in the city this week. I will now hand over the mic to one of our brave officers, Amar Shinde, who will narrate our findings so far."

Amar stepped up to the podium, his expression serious. "Good morning, ladies and gentlemen. Coming straight to the point, we have found three bodies so far. Their faces were completely disfigured, as if the killer wanted to hide their identities, but he failed. Thanks to the biometric records, we were able to identify the bodies through their them. After the post-mortem, we discovered a strange situation with their organs…" He paused, taking a deep breath.

"What did you find?" one of the reporters shouted.

"We found all their organs partially fused into each other, as if they were never distinct," Amar revealed.

"What do you mean? Has the killer done something beyond medical science?", another reporter from the front row argued.

"Yes! I am very sure of what I am saying. The killer has done something that may not be beyond medical science, but it is definitely beyond what we know so far," Amar asserted.

"Fortunately, we have arrested the man we strongly believe is responsible for these murders. This conference is to inform you that we have a suspect in custody and will be interrogating him for his offenses."

"Who is he? Is he Javed Malik?" another reporter asked.

"No! He is not Javed Malik. I assure you of that. We are keeping the identity of the suspect classified until the interrogation ends. I will end my statement here. Before leaving, I request everyone not to believe rumors in such a sensitive situation. Thank you all."

The commissioner announced the end of the conference. Jay exhaled in relief as Amar clarified that the killings were not related to Javed Malik. He quickly made his way to Amar and pulled him aside into the lobby outside the hall, accessible from the front side door of the conference room.

"Who is the killer? For a moment, I was afraid our plan would fail," Jay said, his voice tense.

"I want you to join me in this case. It's a mess; we're dealing with something supernatural," Amar replied.

"What?" Jay asked, incredulous.

"Yes! This is not the right place to talk. Remember our last base? Meet me there in an hour," Amar instructed.

Their conversation was cut short as officers began emptying the stage and coming out into the lobby to return to the police station. Amar was about to leave with the other officers when they suddenly heard screams from the hall. Everyone rushed back in, stunned by what they saw. The same parting line previously noticed on the highway now separated the hall into two. Some members of the crowd were found cut, their blood splattered all over the chairs and tables. The smell of burning flesh added to the horrifying scene.

Reporters and attendees scrambled to find an exit, their faces pale with shock and fear. Some tripped over chairs and each other in their desperate attempt to escape. The once orderly conference room was now a scene of utter pandemonium, with overturned furniture and scattered belongings.

The officers, though trained for emergencies, were visibly shaken. Their voices, usually calm and authoritative, were now tinged with urgency and panic as they tried to direct the crowd to safety.

"Get everyone out, one by one, this way!" an officer shouted, his voice barely audible over the din of frightened cries and the chaotic shuffle of feet.

Amar, amidst the turmoil, tried to maintain his composure. He quickly called Bodke to check on Arjun, his mind racing with the implications of the supernatural event they had just witnessed. Jay, too, was caught in the frenzy, helping to guide people out while keeping an eye on Amar.

The fear was palpable, a heavy weight that pressed down on everyone in the room. The realization that something beyond their understanding and control was at play only heightened the sense of dread. It was a scene of confusion, desperation, and a primal instinct to survive, as everyone grappled with the terrifying reality unfolding before them.

(Distant siren of an ambulance in the background)

Bodke arrived with Arjun, and upon seeing the horrific condition inside the hall, he immediately ran back outside. Amar grabbed Arjun and forcefully pulled him towards the crack in the floor. Arjun, handcuffed with his hands behind his back, felt uncomfortable. He closed his eyes, and in an instant, the handcuffs melted into a molten lava-like substance, freeing his hands. Amar watched in astonishment.

“Look! This is what you did to these people. Seven cuts in half, some lost their limbs. Why did you do this? Answer me!” Amar demanded, his voice filled with anger and confusion.

“First of all, I was in the lockup you put me in. How could I be here and do this? Stop blaming me. I’m as shocked as you are. I’m afraid he will come stronger this time,” Arjun replied, his voice steady but urgent. He then forced Amar to sit and observe the ignited borders around the crack. “Come here. Look. You see this flame? It’s red. A dark, glowing red.”

"What does it mean?" Amar asked, his voice trembling.

"This means Shakhti has returned to Earth, and the person he possessed is not capable of handling his tremendous powers. That's why he is killing everyone," Arjun explained, pulling Amar closer by grabbing his collar. His gaze was intense, piercing into Amar's eyes. "Now listen, don't let anyone enter this hall for some time. I can fix this with my powers. Though it won't solve the problem completely, what I'm going to do can make a difference. Leave now."

Amar left the hall and closed the door from the outside. He tried to calm himself after witnessing Arjun's dominating presence. He had never imagined Arjun could be so dangerous. Amar grabbed a water bottle, opened the cap, and poured the water over his head. He took a sip from the half-filled bottle and then noticed the door being knocked from the inside. Amar rushed to the door and opened it. It was Arjun, knocking with his hands tied with the same handcuffs. Amar looked behind him and what he saw made him lose his balance. An officer rushed to support Amar, helping him stand.

Arjun walked closer to Amar. "Past is now the present," Arjun smirked. "Humans have a lot to learn yet. Your existence is tied to time, and for me," he paused, "TIME IS NOTHING."

Inside the hall, Arjun turned his attention to the gruesome scene. He closed his eyes and began to concentrate. The air around him seemed to shimmer as he channeled his supernatural abilities. Slowly, the severed limbs and bodies began to reassemble. The blood that had splattered across the room started to flow back into the bodies, and the smell of burning flesh dissipated.

The crowd outside the hall watched in awe through the windows as the impossible unfolded before their eyes. Arjun's hands glowed with a soft blue light as he moved them in intricate patterns, guiding the resurrection process. The bodies, once lifeless and mutilated, began to show signs of life. Limbs reattached, wounds healed, and color returned to their faces.

Amar, still reeling from the shock, watched as the dead were brought back to life. He couldn't believe what he was seeing. Arjun's power was beyond anything he had ever imagined. The hall, once a scene of horror, was now filled with the miraculous sight of people being restored.

As the last of the bodies were resurrected, Arjun's glow faded, and he took a deep breath. He turned to Amar; his expression serious. "This is just the beginning. We have much to do, and Shakhti will not stop. We must be prepared for what comes next."

Amar nodded, his mind racing with the implications of what he had just witnessed. The battle against Shakhti was far from over, but with Arjun's powers, they had a fighting chance. Together, they would face the darkness and uncover the truth behind the supernatural events that had turned their lives upside down. Amar was very overwhelmed due the sequence of events he witnessed his mind was in constant turmoil of reporting all events withing the boundaries of constitution.

•••

"From the wreckage, Amar heard the sound of metal scraping. Arjun kicked open the rear door from inside and emerged from the debris. Amar stared at him, noticing his pupils had darkened and enlarged. The crowd saw Arjun's demonic form for the first time and fled in terror. Arjun jumped from the wreck and walked towards Amar, his presence exuding a menacing aura."

CHAPTER **FOUR** EARLY OMENS

Arjun smirked at Amar before striding towards the van parked outside. Bodke, already standing by the van, swiftly forced Arjun inside. Amar, taken aback, watched in astonishment as people began emerging from the hall, alive. The officers beside him were equally amazed. The scene inside the hall was surreal; there were no bloodstains, only a wavy outline of a beam still glowing red.

Once everyone had exited, Amar and two officers rushed inside to check if anyone remained. Suddenly, Amar remembered, “Wait! We took two bodies out in the ambulance. Where are those two reporters?” One of the officers sprinted towards the ambulance and found the two reporters sitting up on the bed, alive. He gave Amar a thumbs-up from a distance.

Meanwhile, Arjun sat quietly in the police van, seemingly unaware of the chaos he had caused. Resurrecting the dead was unheard of until now. Arjun had used his celestial powers to bring them back to life. Fortunately, Jagtapji had not been present during the incident. He arrived at the scene in his car, and his driver, Mangu, quickly opened the rear door for him. Jagtapji stepped out and immediately approached Amar.

“Where is he?” Jagtapji asked in a low, stern voice.

“Inside the van,” Amar replied.

“I need to speak with him. I need to know what happened here,” Jagtapji demanded.

Amar pointed to the van, and Jagtapji entered. The van was a typical police vehicle, fenced on all sides with a face-to-face seating arrangement in the rear. There was a small opening to communicate with the driver, covered by a checkered steel plate. Jagtapji sat down in front of Arjun, who was seated at the end of the bench towards the driver’s side.

“Who are you?” Jagtapji demanded, his voice dripping with authority and impatience.

Arjun locked eyes with Jagtapji, his face a mask of indifference. He remained silent, his gaze unwavering until Jagtapji's powerful, dominating stare bore into him.

"I am not supposed to answer you. I will talk to Amar," Arjun finally replied, his tone defiant.

Jagtapji's face flushed with anger. He stood up abruptly, grabbing Arjun by the shirt and lifting him off the bench. In a swift motion, Arjun broke his handcuffs and shoved Jagtapji back. The older man collided with the side wall of the van, the impact producing a loud thud that caught Bodke's attention outside. Bodke rushed towards the van, but Amar intercepted him, holding him back. Amar wanted Jagtapji to question Arjun about the supernatural act he had performed moments earlier.

Inside the van, Jagtapji regained his footing and pulled Arjun towards him again, gripping his shirt tightly and staring into his eyes. Suddenly, Jagtapji's eyes turned red, and Arjun felt a searing pain in his head. The hidden monster within him threatened to emerge, but he managed to control himself. He loosened his grip on Jagtapji's arms and whispered, "SHAKHTI?"

Jagtapji's confirming nod sent a shiver down Arjun's spine. The one he had feared for years had revealed himself. Jagtapji, now Shakhti, released Arjun's collar and repeated his question,

"Who are you?"

"Venan," Arjun replied, his voice filled with a mix of anger and resignation.

Shakhti placed his right hand on Arjun's shoulder, sensing his son Venan within Arjun's body. Arjun angrily brushed off his hand. "Why are you here? Have you forgotten what gods did to us before?"

"Venan, I came here to find my children. The throne is waiting for you two. I mean no harm to mankind… at least for now," Shakhti said, his voice calm but firm.

"You killed people in the hall," Arjun accused.

"I didn't mean to! It was just an accident," Shakhti paused, "just like an accident killed your mother! But what you did in front of them is truly horrible. You should have considered the consequences of resurrecting people."

"Enough! I remember it wasn't an accident. I am aware of your sweet talks and won't fall for them this time. Now leave me alone!" Arjun yelled, his anger boiling over.

In a fit of rage, Arjun unleashed a plasma beam at Shakhti. Shakhti instantly disappeared, and the plasma beam sliced through the van, hitting other vehicles and causing explosions. The crowd outside was stunned, and people scrambled for cover. Officers rushed to rescue civilians, while Amar ran towards the van to check on Jagtapji.

From the wreckage, Amar heard the sound of metal scraping. Arjun kicked open the rear door from inside and emerged from the debris. Amar stared at him, noticing his pupils had darkened and enlarged. The crowd saw Arjun's demonic form for the first time and fled in terror. Arjun jumped from the wreck and walked towards Amar, his presence exuding a menacing aura.

"Don't fear me. Fear SHAKHTI. He took Jagtapji," Arjun said, his voice steady but ominous.

"What? Where is Jagtapji?" Amar asked, panic rising in his voice as he ran to the wreckage, frantically searching for Jagtapji.

"He is gone! Too far. If Shakhti has him, he is dead," Arjun replied, turning towards Amar. His eyes returned to their normal state.

"Help me! Help me find him," Amar begged, desperation clear in his voice.

"I can't help you, no matter how badly I want to. He is taken by Shakhti. No one has the power to influence what Shakhti manipulates," Arjun said, trying to convince Amar of the hopelessness of the situation.

The loss of Jagtapji hit Amar hard. He collapsed to his knees, crying out in pain. Arjun walked over and placed a hand on his shoulder, but Amar angrily brushed it off. Fueled by rage, Amar stood up, grabbed Arjun, and dragged him to an intact car. He drove him to the interrogation base, with Arjun understanding the emotional turmoil Amar was experiencing and not resisting. Jay, hiding behind a wall, saw Amar driving Arjun away and followed them.

At the interrogation base, Amar pulled Arjun out of the car. Jay arrived shortly after and running over. Amar forced Arjun into a chair, his eyes bloodshot with anger.

"What happened in the van?" Amar demanded.

"Jagtapji tried to kill me," Arjun answered calmly.

"He would never do that during an interrogation," Amar retorted.

"But he wasn't Jagtapji," Arjun paused. "He was Shakhti. I've been running from him for ages, and he found me here."

"Who is he?" Amar asked, his curiosity piqued.

"Shakhti, my brother Beran, and I are demons. We inhabit the bodies of living beings and possess celestial powers. We manipulate the universe, time, and matter. Shakhti is the most powerful among us. We've existed since long before this planet was created," Arjun explained.

"Humans believe the Big Bang created the universe. It wasn't the Big Bang; it was us. When two supreme celestial powers collided, it created this beautiful universe. Both gods and demons realized these powers could destroy everything we had, so we pledged not to fight. We divided eras to rule the remains of Celestious. Amon, one of the gods, slowed down the time of all the exploding pieces of Celestious."

"Celestious?" Amar asked, intrigued.

"It was the most amazing place we had," Arjun smiled at the memory. "It was the world we lived in, a gigantic form of your universe. It's beyond your imagination. Everything was fine until the celestials divided into two groups: gods and demons. We all had equal powers, but it's not the power that makes you a god or a demon; it's the purpose you use them for. Gods wanted equality for all, while demons wanted to dominate and rule over Celestious. I never wanted this. The friction increased, and the supremes from both sides raised their deadliest weapons, leading to the splitting of Celestious. Its pieces turned into small universes. The supreme god ordered Amon to slow down the destruction. Gods developed the ability to combine their powers before the great war. They started to kill us, but we survived. Shakhti was a favorite of the supreme demon. Gods killed our leader and acquired his powers. Shakhti is the last of the supremes, and unfortunately, I am his creation."

"Where are the gods now?" Amar asked.

"They are among us. We are spread across all universes. The supreme still holds Celestious, which is slowly breaking down," Arjun replied.

"Slowly?" Amar questioned.

"The breakdown will end after billions and billions of years," Arjun said, his voice trailing off as he looked into the distance, lost in thought.

"How big is Celestious?" Amar asked, his voice steady but filled with curiosity.

Arjun leaned back in his chair, a faint smile playing on his lips. "Particles flew out of Celestious after the collision and created your universe. You are smart enough to imagine its size."

Amar glanced at Jay, who stepped forward. "What is your real form?" Jay asked, his tone demanding.

"This is who I am in reality. Arjun. The gods took everything we had. Now we are all souls without bodies," Arjun sighed. "Jagtap is dead by now. SHAKTI has taken him."

"Where is he now?" Amar's voice wavered with concern.

"I don't know. But I warn you, don't focus on Jagtap being dead. There is something bigger waiting for you, something the whole world couldn't imagine," Arjun replied, his tone grave.

Amar dragged a chair closer to Arjun, his frustration boiling over. "Why are you keeping us in the dark? We lost men hours ago. I lost my best mentor. Do you think this is a joke?" he yelled.

Arjun leaned towards Amar, his expression serious. "No, but I am concerned about something else. If SHAKTI is here, all of mankind could vanish in the blink of an eye."

"So, you fight and kill him, problem solved", Jay suggested.

"No, It's not that easy. We need him for one big objective", Arjun said.

"What is it?", Amar asked.

"Eventually everything will be revealed", Arjun Said.

Jay stood still, absorbing Arjun's words. Amar glanced at Jay, then stood up, running a hand through his hair before turning back to Arjun. "What can we do to stop him? What do we have?"

"Me," Arjun smirked.

Just then, Jay's phone rang. He answered it, listening intently. "Javed is in the city. I have to leave, need to keep tabs on him to execute my plan to kill him," Jay whispered to Amar.

"If you allow me, I can do it for you," Arjun interjected.

"You stay out of it. I'll handle it my way. Amar, you take care of him," Jay instructed before leaving.

Amar grabbed a bottle of water from the table, walked out to refill it, and returned to find Arjun gone. "SHIT!" he yelled, throwing the bottle and banging the table in frustration.

Police Station - Later

Amar droves back to the police station, where he learned that CCTV footage had leaked to the media, showing blurry visuals of Jagtap and Arjun in the van. Bodke approached Amar, showing him the footage. Jagtapji's eyes glowed red, and his face was covered with glowing red lines, resembling lava shining through cracks in rock.

"Jagtapji is no more. His body is taken by a demon called SHAKTI. He has come here to annihilate mankind," Amar stated, his voice heavy with the weight of the revelation.

The room fell silent, the officers stunned. Nikam switched the TV to various news channels, all flashing the conference news. The public was in panic, with reports escalating to the resurrection of dead people.

"Sir, we are all tired of answering their questions. Soon, we are going to have a visitor. The Chief Minister," Nikam informed Amar.

Amar sighed, walking slowly to his cabin, feeling completely overwhelmed by the situation. Minutes later, a convoy of cars stopped outside the police station. The Chief Minister of Maharashtra arrived, accompanied by the current police commissioner and senior officers, ready to meet with Amar.

The room was tense as the Chief Minister (CM) entered Amar's cell, his face stern. "What is happening in the city? Do you even have an idea?" he demanded.

"Sir, we've witnessed things that are beyond belief in a very short period. We had someone who we thought could help us, but now he's disappeared from the interrogation base," Amar explained, his voice strained.

The CM pulled back a typical wooden chair and sat down, motioning for Amar to do the same. Meanwhile, the commissioner handed over some CCTV snapshots showing Jagtap with glowing red eyes. "This isn't new to you. We've seen this footage on TV. Can you tell me what it is?" the commissioner asked.

"Jagtap is possessed by a demon called SHAKHTI. The one in the photo is not Jagtap; he's no more. And..." Amar paused, gathering his thoughts. "The one we arrested is Venan. He has Arjun's body. Both of them are demons."

"What rubbish is this? You don't even sound like a police officer," the CM retorted, disbelief evident in his voice.

"Sir, I've already told you we are dealing with something that is hard to believe. Venan told us this. He's the one who resurrected people. He seems to be on our side for now, but I don't trust him," Amar replied.

"Where is he now?" the CM asked.

"Disappeared in the middle of the interrogation," Amar said, frustration creeping into his voice. Suddenly, Arjun entered the cabin, smiling at Amar before sitting on the second chair beside the CM. "Ohh!! Stop staring at me!" he said, a smirk on his face.

"Where were you?" Amar stood up; his voice sharp.

"Somewhere SHAKHTI can't find me," Arjun replied, sighing as he looked at the CM. "Oh, don't be surprised. I know Amar told you about me."

The CM took out his handkerchief to wipe his forehead, but Arjun waved his hand, and the sweat instantly steamed.

"Are you really a demon?" the CM asked, his voice trembling.

"Yes, I am. One of the deadliest you might have seen in movies," Arjun replied calmly.

"You're scaring him," Amar argued.

"He should be scared of me. Everyone should. After all, I am the third most powerful demon alive," Arjun said, his tone matter-of-fact.

The CM stood up, taking a step back. "Don't worry, I won't hurt any of you. Calm down!" Arjun said in a soothing voice. "SHAKHTI is here to annihilate mankind. I am not with him and never will be. I would rather help you stop him."

"You said he is the most powerful among you three. How are you going to stop him?" Amar asked.

"I can because Amon is here too. Amon has saved this planet before, and I am sure if we find him, we can definitely fight SHAKHTI," Arjun explained.

"Who is Amon?" the CM questioned.

"You will know… you will know. For now, leave us alone. I trust Amar; we will figure things out," Arjun said.

Feeling both insulted and afraid, the CM left with his team. He instructed to handle media carefully and Arjun gazed at Amar and smiled.

#

Same Evening - Near Javed Ustad's birthday venue.

Jay and his team waited for Javed Ustad to arrive at his house. They managed to capture some visuals of Javed on their cameras.

"Shaurya, have you practiced well?" Jay asked.

"Yes, sir. I will make sure this parcel is placed properly so we can hear the insights of his meeting," Shaurya replied confidently.

Javed Ustad had invited his friends from India for his birthday party. Although they were celebrating two days early, many known criminals attended the meet. Javed entered the hall in disguise. His usually clean-shaven face was covered with a fake long beard, and he wore a yellow suit. His only identification was his right hand; Javed had lost a finger in a combat with the police once and used to wear a prosthetic finger, which was easy to spot.

Party Hall - Javed Ustad's Residence

Shaurya infiltrated the party, posing as a security guard for one of the criminals. He discreetly placed a gift near the table where he was certain Javed would sit. Moments later, two men entered the hall and ordered everyone to leave, except for a select few.

"Shaurya? Copy?" Jay's voice crackled through the earpiece.

"Sir, they've ordered us to leave the hall now," Shaurya whispered, his voice barely audible through the cleverly concealed microphone in his collar.

"Why?" Jay inquired; his tone sharp.

"Javed is about to start the meeting. They've filtered out some people among us. All of them are wearing red ties. We're heading out now. Signing off," Shaurya responded, maintaining his composure.

Shaurya communicated with Jay, who was stationed in a secure van outside the party location. Jay watched as Shaurya and several others exited the main hall and took seats on a couch outside. Jay instructed one of his officers to activate the wireless camera hidden in the gift Shaurya had placed earlier. The camera provided a clear view of the party hall.

A short while later, one of the men welcomed Javed into the hall. Javed, dressed in a suit, removed his fake beard and wiped the remaining adhesive from his cheeks. He walked to the designated chair and sat down, crossing his right leg over his left knee.

"After so long, we have all gathered together. I believe this bond will never weaken among us," Javed began, pausing for effect. "I will ensure you enjoy the party after I make two significant announcements. First, I have successfully taken control of three large oil fields in Syria and am collaborating with the Islamic State for upcoming activities in Pakistan."

A group of eight people applauded Javed's announcement. "Hold your applause for the second announcement," Javed continued. "I withdrawing myself from all my businesses in India."

The hall erupted in murmurs of surprise. Javed raised his left hand to silence them. "I know you are all surprised. Let me finish. All my businesses in India will now be managed by Mr. Akabar Khaan."

A bearded man walked in, and Jay, inside the surveillance van, tried to focus on his face. "I know this guy. He's one of the leaders associated with IS. There will be serious consequences if he's here," Jay muttered to his colleagues.

"Shaurya, copy! Shaurya!" Jay tried to reconnect with Shaurya.

"Sir, Shaurya's transmitter is not responding," the officer beside Jay reported.

"Try accessing the hotel's CCTV channels," Jay ordered.

The officer attempted a connection to the hotel's CCTV but failed. "Negative!"

"Keep trying. Something's happened to Shaurya. I need to go in and find him," Jay said, grabbing his gun and sliding it into his belt at the back. He donned his jacket to conceal the weapon.

A gentle beep confirmed connection with CCTV in corridor. Where he saw Shaurya is being dragged in room.

Jay held back to seeing two live feeds from CCTV and Spy Cam.

Jay's heart pounded as he watched the live feed from the camera. "He's about to slaughter Shaurya at the party," Jay exclaimed. "Keep reporting what's happening in the hall."

Jay exited the van, with a loaded gun, and sprinted towards the gate. He fired two rounds at the guards stationed outside the party hall. The sudden gunfire startled the criminals, who quickly drew their weapons and returned fire. The ensuing shootout disrupted Javed's meeting, putting Khaan on high alert. Jay's officer reported that Shaurya was being dragged back into the room and that some of the men were preparing their automatic weapons to protect Khaan and Javed.

"Call for backup!" Jay ordered, taking cover behind a three-foot compound wall outside the hotel. The hotel's simple construction offered few hiding places. The corridor, lined with glass, provided a clear view of the waiting couches inside.

Jay found a secure spot from which he could take out his targets without being seen. He retrieved a suppressor from his jacket, attached it to his gun, and took aim at one of the gunmen. Jay wanted to confuse attackers so he used suppressed round in order to avoid being noticed where the fire is coming from. A single shot rang out, and the man collapsed. The thud of the body hitting the ground alerted another gunman, who rushed to his fallen comrade, scanning the surroundings in panic.

Jay seized the opportunity and fired, the bullet piercing the second gunman's eye.

"Sir, Khaan is leaving through the back of the hotel. Javed is with him too," the officer reported.

"Javed isn't important now. Khaan is the one I need alive," Jay replied, his voice tense.

As Jay communicated through his transmitter, a man grabbed him from behind, snatching his gun. "Here you are. Come with me," the man growled, dragging Jay towards Khaan's car and shoving him inside.

Inside the car, Jay found Shaurya already seated, unconscious. One of Khaan's men struck Jay hard across the face, causing him to lose consciousness.

#

Two days later- Kritika's Clinic

Kritika sat in her cozy counseling room, the afternoon sun casting a warm glow through the window. The room smelled faintly of lavender—a deliberate choice to soothe her patients. Today, she was about to meet Grishma, a weary woman seeking solace from her relentless nightmares.

The door opened, and Grishma stepped in—a 30-year-old with haunted eyes. Kritika welcomed her with a genuine smile, hoping to ease her distress. "Hi! Please have a seat," she gestured toward the plush armchair.

"Thank you," Grishma replied, sinking into the chair. "I've been waiting for you. These dreams…" Her voice trailed off, and Kritika noticed the tension in her shoulders.

Kritika leaned forward, her empathy palpable. "Tell me about these dreams, Grishma. What do you see?"

Grishma hesitated, then spoke softly. "It's always the same—a tall man, bathed in red light. He emits something, and I find myself standing before him. The fear is overwhelming. And then…" She shuddered. "I touch that red beam, and everything goes dark."

Kritika furrowed her brow. "Have you ever encountered anything like this in real life? Maybe in a movie or a story?"

Grishma shook her head. "No, never. It's as if my mind conjured this nightmare out of thin air."

Kritika considered her options. "Grishma, these dreams might be linked to something deeper—a trauma perhaps. I suspect it's post-traumatic stress disorder (PTSD). But don't worry; we'll work through this together." She jotted down a prescription for Grishma, hoping it would bring her some relief.

As Grishma left, Kritika's phone buzzed. It was Dr. Abhishek, a colleague from Navi Mumbai. His voice crackled urgently through the line. "Kritika, something strange is happening. I've dismissed three patients with identical dream patterns—a red figure, fear, and darkness. No apparent connection between them."

Kritika's curiosity piqued. "Abhishek, that's uncanny! I had a similar case just now."

"Seriously!" Abhishek's voice held a mix of concern and intrigue. "We need answers. Hypnotherapy, perhaps?"

Kritika nodded, even though Abhishek couldn't see her. "Agreed. Let's dig deeper. And speaking of patients, my assistant just mentioned another one with creepy dream patterns. Shall I see them?"

"Absolutely," Abhishek replied. "Let's unravel this mystery together."

And so, in the quiet of her counseling room, Dr. Kritika prepared to meet yet another dream-weary soul.

Little did she know that these recurring nightmares held secrets that transcended individual minds—a crimson thread connecting them all.

Dr. Kritika's counseling room seemed to absorb the weight of countless whispered fears. As Manish stepped inside, his eyes—tired, haunted—swept over the room. The air held a tension that only those who grappled with nightmares could truly understand.

"Come in," Kritika's voice was gentle, inviting. She watched as Manish settled into the observation chair, his fingers tracing invisible patterns on the armrest. His gaze darted from the framed diplomas on the wall to the potted plant in the corner, seeking refuge from the unspoken dread.

"Hi," Kritika said, her smile a lifeline. "I'm Dr. Kritika. You're Manish, right?"

Manish nodded; his voice barely audible. "Yes. Manish."

Kritika leaned forward, her eyes kind. "Manish, tell me about these dreams. The ones that haunt you."

He hesitated, then began. "A reddish glow—a god, I think. But not a benevolent one. No, this deity emanates menace. I find myself standing before it, paralyzed. And then…" His voice cracked. "I die. Every time. My heart races, and I wake up drenched in sweat."

Kritika's mind raced. The crimson figure—the same as Grishma's and the others. What cosmic force wove their nightmares together?

"Manish," she said, "these dreams might be your mind's way of processing something deeper. Perhaps a trauma you've buried."

He looked lost. "But I can't remember anything traumatic."

"Sometimes," Kritika explained, "our minds shield us from painful memories. They wrap them in dreams, hoping we'll unravel the truth when we're ready."

She wrote a prescription, her pen scratching against paper. "Take these. They'll help ease the intensity. And consider hypnotherapy—it might reveal what your waking mind conceals."

Manish stood, clutching the prescription. "Thank you, Dr. Kritika."

As he left, Kritika stared at the crimson thread connecting her patients. What ancient tale did it whisper? And how many more souls would seek her solace, their dreams woven into a shared nightmare?

And so, in the quiet of her counseling room, Dr. Kritika waited—for the next dreamer, the next chapter in this enigmatic saga. Kritika's phone buzzed, interrupting her contemplation of the crimson thread that bound her patients' nightmares. She glanced at the screen—it was Dr. Abhishek. Urgent, as always.

"Hello?" she answered, her voice steady.

"Kritika," Abhishek's words tumbled out, "I need you to brace yourself. Remember those three patients with the recurring dreams? The ones we thought were connected?"

"Yes," Kritika replied, her curiosity piqued. "What's happened?"

"They're reporters," Abhishek said. "All three of them attended a conference two days ago. It was supposed to be about near-death experiences, consciousness, and the unexplained."

Kritika leaned forward, her mind racing. "And?"

Abhishek's voice dropped to a whisper. "During the conference, something inexplicable occurred. A panel of mystics demonstrated a ritual—a resurrection ritual. They claimed it was by a demonic entity. But Kritika, the reporters who attended? They're alive—fully alive."

Kritika's pulse quickened. "Resurrected? How?"

"I don't know," Abhishek admitted. "But they're different. Changed. Their eyes hold secrets, and their dreams…" He hesitated. "Their dreams mirror what they witnessed during the ritual."

Kritika's thoughts spun. "The crimson figure—the figure they saw in their nightmares?"

"Yes," Abhishek confirmed. "And there's more. They remember fragments—ancient symbols, whispered chants. It's as if they glimpsed beyond mortality."

"What do we do?" Kritika asked, her mind shifting into problem-solving mode.

"We meet them," Abhishek said. "Together. We explore their memories, their dreams. Maybe they hold answers—about the shared nightmare, about the crimson god."

Kritika stood, her heart pounding. "I'll be there. But Abhishek, what if—"

"—what if we're unraveling something forbidden?" he finished. "I know. But we're on the edge of understanding, Kritika. And sometimes, understanding requires stepping into the abyss."

As they hung up, Kritika stared at the crimson thread, now woven with threads of resurrection. The veil between dreams and reality had frayed, and she was about to step through.

And so, in the quiet of her counseling room, Dr. Kritika prepared for a journey beyond science, beyond sanity—a quest fueled by shared nightmares and the promise of revelation.

Her phone buzzes

#

In the dim, shadowy room, the air was thick with tension. The sound of heavy footsteps echoed as a man approached the two figures slumped in wooden chairs, their heads drooping under the weight of unconsciousness. With a swift motion, he yanked the black cloths off their faces, revealing Shaurya and Jay, both heavily drugged, their eyes barely able to adjust to the sudden light. Shaurya's head lolled as he struggled to regain full consciousness, his body weak and unresponsive to his desperate attempts to move.

"Stop squirming, you idiot!" barked one of Khan's men, his voice laced with irritation as he glared at Shaurya.

Two more men entered the room; their faces set with grim determination. As the door creaked shut behind them, Shaurya blinked rapidly, trying to shake off the drug-induced haze. Jay stirred next to him, slowly coming to, his eyes filled with confusion as he realized he was bound tightly to a chair. Shaurya, gaining a fraction more clarity, turned his head toward Jay, his heart pounding as he tried to wake his partner.

One of the men opened a small, metal box, revealing a syringe and a vial, the tools they would use to force the two back into oblivion if necessary. The second man dragged a wooden stool across the floor, the screeching sound reverberating through the room. He positioned it directly in front of Shaurya and sat down, his gaze cold and piercing.

"I have to hand it to you," the man said, his voice dripping with sarcasm. "It takes guts to walk into the lion's den, thinking you could actually capture Javed. But you should have done your homework, boys. You're not leaving this room until you tell me everything. What's your plan?"

Shaurya shook his head weakly, refusing to give in. The man's expression darkened, and without warning, he delivered a brutal punch to Shaurya's face. Blood trickled from Shaurya's lip as he recoiled in pain, but he remained silent.

Jay, still groggy but now fully aware of the situation, strained against his chains, his heart racing as he watched his partner take the beating. Seeing Jay's struggle, the man turned his attention to him, slapping him hard across the face.

"Stay quiet!" he shouted, drawing a sleek, black Beretta from his belt. He aimed it directly at Jay's head, his eyes narrowed with deadly intent. "One wrong move, and you'll regret."

Jay froze, his body tense with fear, as the man turned back to Shaurya, his fury barely contained.

"You bastard!" he snarled, his voice rising with each word. "Tell me, what was your plan? And who the hell is behind this operation?"

Shaurya's vision blurred with pain, but he managed to speak, his voice hoarse and strained. "No one," he whispered, his resolve unbroken despite the torment.

Behind the scenes, Javed and Khan were on edge. They knew their illicit activities were being scrutinized by corrupt politicians and ministers within the Indian government—individuals who had once been their allies but were now plotting against them. Just two months prior, one of Javed's men had killed the son of a powerful minister in Tamil Nadu over a dispute concerning their cut of the profits. The fallout from that incident had led to this intensified scrutiny, and now, they were desperate to uncover who within the government was orchestrating this operation.

Javed's anxiety was heightened by the knowledge that he had successfully smuggled 300 kilograms of RDX into Sri Lanka, with plans to transport it into India for a series of devastating attacks. The operation was critical, and any slip-up that alerted the Indian government could spell disaster, not just for him, but for ISIS, who were planning simultaneous bombings in seven major cities across India.

Despite the pain coursing through his body, Shaurya refused to betray his mission.

"No one," he repeated.

As the man's furious demand hung in the air, Jay's mind raced. Despite the throbbing pain in his head and the haze of the drugs still coursing through his system, a single thought took root: they needed to get out, or at the very least, buy some time. His hands remained tightly bound, but he felt a slight looseness around his right ankle. The ropes binding his legs were not as tight as they should have been, probably hastily tied by one of Khan's less experienced men.

Jay stayed perfectly still, careful not to draw attention to himself. The man holding the Beretta was focused on Shaurya, pressing him for answers with increasing frustration. The other men hovered close; their attention fixed on the interrogation. This was his moment.

Slowly, deliberately, Jay began to twist his foot, inching it back and forth in tiny, imperceptible movements. Each subtle shift loosened the rope a fraction more, but he had to be patient. If he moved too quickly, he would be caught, and there would be no second chances.

Meanwhile, Shaurya continued to bear the brunt of the man's anger. His face was bruised, blood trickling from the corner of his mouth, but he met the man's gaze with unwavering defiance. "I said… no one," Shaurya repeated, his voice barely above a whisper, but laced with a resolve that only angered their captors further.

"You think this is a game?" the man roared, raising his fist for another strike. "You think I won't—"

Before he could finish, Jay acted. With a final twist, he freed his right leg, the rope falling away silently. He wasted no time. In one fluid motion, he kicked out hard, knocking the stool out from under the interrogator. The man tumbled to the floor with a grunt, his gun skidding across the room.

For a split second, chaos reigned. The two other men lunged towards Jay, but he was already on his feet, using the element of surprise to his advantage. With his hands still tied, Jay launched himself at the nearest man, driving his shoulder into the thug's midsection, forcing the air from his lungs in a pained wheeze. They crashed into the table, sending the box with the syringe and vial clattering to the floor.

"Shaurya!" Jay shouted, trying to give his partner a moment to recover. But Shaurya was too weakened from the beatings and the drugs, his movements sluggish as he struggled against his own bonds.

The second man, quicker and stronger, grabbed Jay by the neck, slamming him against the wall. Jay fought back with everything he had, bringing his knee up into the man's stomach, but it wasn't enough. The man recovered quickly, his grip tightening around Jay's throat, cutting off his air.

The man Jay had tackled was already back on his feet, his face twisted in rage. He grabbed a heavy metal pipe from a nearby table, raising it high with murder in his eyes. With a desperate burst of energy, Jay kicked out again, this time at the man holding him, but it wasn't enough to break free.

The pipe came down hard, striking Jay across the back. Pain exploded through his body, and his legs buckled beneath him. The second blow came swiftly, this time to his side, sending him sprawling to the ground, gasping for breath.

The man who had been interrogating Shaurya picked himself up, fury etched into every line of his face. He stalked over to Jay, who was now on the floor, struggling to breathe. "You thought you could escape, huh? You thought you were clever?" he sneered, wiping the blood from his split lip. He retrieved his gun, which had fallen just out of reach, and aimed it squarely at Jay's head.

Shaurya, still bound and barely able to move, watched helplessly as his partner was beaten. The room spun around him, but he fought to stay conscious, to find some way, anyway, to help.

The man with the gun cocked the hammer, his finger hovering over the trigger. "This is what happens when you mess with Khan," he spat.

Just as he was about to pull the trigger, the door to the room flew open with a crash, and a loud voice barked,

"Stop!"

Khan himself strode in, exuding a menacing calm that instantly silenced the room. He looked from Jay, battered and bloodied on the floor, to Shaurya, who was barely holding on to consciousness. His cold, calculating eyes narrowed as he took in the scene.

"Not yet," Khan said in a low, deadly voice. "They have information we need. Finish them off after they've talked." He turned to his men; his voice as sharp as a blade. "Get him back on that chair. And this time, make sure both stays tied down."

The men obeyed immediately, dragging Jay's limp form back to the chair and tightening the ropes around his legs and arms. Shaurya was shoved roughly back into position, his head lolling forward, but he could still hear, still feel every agonizing moment.

As Jay's vision blurred, the last thing he saw was the smirk on Khan's face as he walked out of the room, leaving them at the mercy of his henchmen. The fight had been valiant, but it had only delayed the inevitable. Now, both officers were back in the hands of their captors, and the real nightmare was about to begin. Moments ago, Khan entered the room back again and angrily approached both.

Khan's eyes gleamed with twisted satisfaction as he leaned forward, snatching the gun from his subordinate's holster. The sound of the weapon's metallic click resonated in the dimly lit room, amplifying the tension. He turned it over in his hands with a casual, almost leisurely motion before aiming it directly at Shaurya's knee. Shaurya, battered and barely conscious, could do nothing but watch in horror as the barrel aligned with his leg.

With a cruel smirk, Khan pulled the trigger.

The gunshot echoed loudly, cutting through the silence. Shaurya screamed in agony, the pain searing through his leg like wildfire. Blood spilled from the wound, soaking through his pants, and he slumped forward, his face contorted in sheer torment.

Khan, completely unmoved by the suffering he'd inflicted, turned his attention to Jay. Jay's eyes were wide with shock and fear, but behind them was a glimmer of recognition. He had seen someone like this before, once—a man with extraordinary powers, someone who had intervened in a situation that had seemed hopeless. Could it be the same person?

Khan noticed Jay's hesitation and sneered. "You, asshole," he spat, his voice dripping with malice. "Your friend seems a bit thick-skinned, but if you don't want him to suffer more, you'd better start talking. Tell me everything."

Khan, sensing Jay's internal struggle, raised the gun to Shaurya's head with deliberate menace. "Three... Two..."

"Nooo!!" Jay's voice cracked with desperation, but Khan was unrelenting. The trigger pulled back, and the gun fired.

Everything seemed to slow down. The gunshot, the flash of the muzzle, the bullet spiraling toward Shaurya's head—it all unfolded in agonizingly slow motion. But just before the bullet could reach its mark, it shattered into thousands of tiny fragments, disintegrating harmlessly into the air. Shaurya, though weakened, was untouched.

Khan's expression shifted from smug satisfaction to shock and confusion. He blinked, momentarily disoriented, trying to make sense of what had just happened. The room, which had been deadly silent moments before, now buzzed with a faint, ominous hum. The lights above began to flicker, casting erratic shadows across the walls.

Before anyone could react, a sudden, powerful gust of wind surged through the room. It was an unnatural force; unlike anything they had ever experienced. One of Khan's men was lifted off his feet and flung into the wall with a sickening crash, his body vanishing through the shattered surface.

Khan and his remaining men staggered backward, their eyes wide with fear, weapons at the ready as they frantically scanned the room. "What the hell…?" one of them muttered, but his words were swallowed by another fierce gust of wind. This time, a blur of blue flame accompanied the wind, streaking past them like a bolt of lightning. It seized another one of Khan's men and hurled him through the opposite wall with terrifying force.

Jay's heart raced as he recognized the signs. The blue flame, the supernatural force—this was Arjun. It had to be. He had seen this power once before, in a situation that was just as dire.

The third gust of wind came without warning, swirling around the remaining men like a vortex. The blue flame grew more distinct, taking on a vaguely human form as it swept through them with brutal efficiency. The last of Khan's henchmen were lifted off the ground, their bodies colliding with a bone-crunching force before being flung aside like ragdolls. The flame subsided, leaving Jay and Shaurya alone with Khan.

Khan, drenched in sweat, his bravado shattered, backed away in fear. His mind raced, searching for an escape, but there was none. The door, his only way out, vanished before his eyes, the wood and metal dissolving into the wall as if it had never existed. Panic gripped him as he realized he was trapped.

Shaurya and Jay, though still bound, could sense the shift in the air. The fear on Khan's face told them that whatever was happening, it was something far beyond the reach of any normal threat.

Khan, his voice shaking, called out, "Who's there? What's happening?"

Before he could gather his thoughts, a figure began to emerge from the corner of the room. Not through the door or a shadow, but from the very wall itself. The surface rippled like water, and through it stepped a young man, his form solidifying as he moved into the room. His eyes glowed with an otherworldly light, and his presence radiated a calm but terrifying power.

"Arjun..." Jay whispered, his voice a mix of relief and disbelief. He didn't know much about him, but he knew enough to feel a sliver of hope.

Arjun's expression remained calm as he acknowledged Jay, but his focus quickly returned to Khan. "You must be Khan," he said, his voice echoing unnaturally in the confined space. He took a step closer; his gaze locked on the trembling criminal. "Why don't you join your men in hell and tell them this is what happens when someone messes with my people."

Khan's eyes widened in sheer terror. "Arjun... no... please forgive me..."

But Arjun didn't wait for a response. With a simple gesture, the air around Khan began to warp and twist. Khan felt an invisible force seize him, lifting him off the ground. He struggled, kicking and thrashing, but it was no use. The force was overwhelming, and it pulled him inexorably toward the same wall through which Arjun had entered.

"No! No! This isn't happening!" Khan screamed, his voice rising in desperation as he was dragged toward the wall. But his pleas fell on deaf ears. The wall rippled once more, and with a final, violent surge, it swallowed Khan whole. His scream was cut off abruptly as the wall solidified behind him, leaving the room eerily quiet once more.

Shaurya and Jay stared in stunned silence, still processing what had just occurred. Their breathing was ragged, and they exchanged a look filled with a mix of fear, awe, and relief. Arjun turned to face them, his expression softening as he approached.

"You're safe now," Arjun said, his voice returning to its normal tone, reassuring but still carrying that edge of power. He knelt beside Shaurya, his hand hovering over the wound in his knee. A soft blue glow emanated from his palm, and as it touched Shaurya's leg, the pain began to fade, the wound closing before their eyes.

Jay, still dazed but immensely grateful, managed to speak. "You saved us!"

Arjun stood amidst the remnants of the battle, the devastation surrounding them weighing heavily on his heart. The once peaceful landscape was now scarred by the violence that had taken place, the air thick with the scent of destruction. His eyes, filled with a deep sadness, scanned the horizon, knowing that danger still lurked nearby.

"We need to leave this place before others arrive," Arjun said, his voice resolute yet laced with sorrow. "I don't want more bloodshed here."

Jay and Shaurya, standing beside him, nodded in agreement. They knew the truth in Arjun's words—lingering any longer would only invite more chaos. Together, they closed their eyes. The world around them blurred and, in the blink of an eye, they vanished from the room, leaving behind only a whisper of their presence.

In the next moment, they reappeared in the warmth and safety of Jay's home. The room was a sanctuary, bathed in the soft glow of lamps, the air filled with the calming scent of incense. It was a stark contrast to the scene they had just left, offering a much-needed reprieve from the horrors of events.

Kritika and Amar, who had been anxiously awaiting their return, immediately rushed toward them. The relief on their faces was palpable, but it was Kritika who reached Jay first. She threw her arms around him, her eyes brimming with tears.

"I was so scared, Jay," Kritika whispered, her voice trembling with emotion. "I couldn't bear the thought of losing you."

Jay held her tightly, his own emotions finally breaking through the stoic facade he had worn during the fight. "I'm here, Kritika. I'm safe because of Arjun. I don't know why women need a now or never situation to admit they can't lose you."

Kritika pulled back slightly, her hands cupping Jay's face as she searched his eyes.

"Better late than never. Promise me you'll be careful. I can't lose you."

Jay nodded, his voice soft and sincere. "I promise."

Nearby, Amar approached Arjun, his expression filled with gratitude. "Thank you, Arjun," he said, his voice thick with emotion. "You saved Jay and Shaurya. I don't know what we'd do without you."

Arjun, still carrying the weight of his decisions, gave Amar a solemn nod. "We're in this together, Amar. I'd do anything to protect them, to protect all of you. In return I seek favor to defeat Shakhti."

Shaurya, sensing the gravity of the moment, placed a hand on Arjun's shoulder. "We owe you our lives, I don't know who you are but eventually will. I'll help you."

As the group settled into the comforting safety of Jay's home, the tension from past two days began to slowly fade. However, the relief was short-lived. Arjun's expression remained grave, a reminder that their ordeal was far from over.

He turned to the others, his voice firm but filled with concern. "Now, we should be focusing on what is coming, and we can't let our guard down. Shakhti is still out there, and he's a threat unlike anything we've ever faced. He won't stop until he's brought devastation to all mankind."

The room fell into a heavy silence, each person grappling with the reality of what lay ahead. Arjun continued; his gaze steady as it swept across his companions. "We need to stay vigilant. Together, we have a chance, but we must be prepared for whatever Shakhti might unleash. The fate of mankind depends on it."

Jay, Kritika, and Amar absorbed his words, the weight of their mission pressing down on them. But Arjun wasn't finished. He took a deep breath, knowing that their next steps were crucial.

"There's something else we need to do," Arjun said, his tone growing more urgent. "We can't defeat Shakhti on our own. His power is beyond anything we can handle by ourselves. There's only one being who might stand a chance against him—Amon, the God Soul. Amon holds the power to banish darkness, even the likes of Shakhti."

Kritika looked up, uncertainty clouding her eyes. "Amon? But... no one knows where to find him. He's been lost for centuries."

Arjun nodded; the gravity of the situation clears in his expression. "I know. But we have to try. Even though no one has any clue where Amon might be, we can't give up. We need to start searching—every legend, every myth, every scrap of information that could lead us to him. He's our only hope."

Amar, despite the daunting task ahead, stepped forward with determination. "I'll start gathering whatever information I can. We might not have any leads now, but we'll find something. We have to."

Jay, holding Kritika's hand, met Arjun's gaze with resolve. "We'll do whatever it takes. We'll find Amon, even if we have to search every corner of the earth."

Arjun looked at each of them, feeling a renewed sense of purpose. "We're in this together. We'll find Amon, and when we do, we'll bring the fight to Shakhti."

The group exchanged determined looks; their fears tempered by a shared commitment. The road ahead would be long and perilous, and the uncertainty of finding Amon loomed over them. But they knew they had no other choice. The battle might have ended, but the war was far from over. Shakhti's shadow threatened their future, but with Amon's help, they might just be able to push back the darkness.

With their mission clear, they began to plan their search, each of them silently vowing to do whatever it took to find Amon and save the world from Shakhti's wrath.

Amar advances, his brow furrowed with a mix of determination and unease. "What does Shakti want from us?" he asks, his voice barely hiding the urgency.

Arjun pauses for a moment, his gaze distant as if staring into the abyss of the knowledge he carries. "Home," he finally says, his tone heavy with the weight of the truth. "Shakti wants a home."

Amar's confusion deepens. "Home?"

Arjun nods slowly, then elaborates, his voice taking on a darker edge. "The demons left behind, the ones we've been fighting—they're just shells, empty husks. They're lost souls, remnants of what they once were. But Shakti... He's something far more dangerous. He doesn't just want to destroy mankind; he wants to assimilate it. Shakti will turn every last human into a demon, and then he will rule this planet as his dominion. After destruction of Celest. If unfortunately, he succeeds in killing Amoon, Celestious will split into many galaxies, multiplying the empire. Every galaxy has several planets to create life and all those lives have unique powers. Shakti will rule every one of them."

Jay, ever the skeptic, interrupts. "But if he's so powerful, why doesn't he just create his own planet? Why go through all this trouble?"

Arjun chuckles, though the sound is devoid of humor. "Now you're sounding like an officer, Jay," he says, shaking his head slightly. "You're thinking with logic, with reason. But listen carefully—there are things that go beyond the boundaries of science, things that defy our understanding of the universe. One of those things is the force that binds the human soul to its body."

He leans in closer, his voice dropping to a near whisper, making the weight of his words even more palpable. "There are invisible forces at play, forces that make your material body function according to the will of your non-material soul. Demons... they have the power to disrupt that balance. They can replace the soul within a body or seize control of both the soul and the body without causing harm to the soul itself. It may seem like an immense power, but it's a twisted one. You see, we cannot create souls. That's beyond even Shakti. But what he can do is corrupt them, twist them to his will. The more souls he gathers under his control, the more powerful he becomes."

Arjun's eyes darken as he continues, "Shakti doesn't just want power; he wants allegiance. He wants every human soul to work as his ally, to fight for his cause. By turning humans into demons, he's not just unlocking their potential—he's bending it to serve his own ends. He'll unlock every biological limitation, every dormant power within their souls, but only so they can serve him more completely."

The weight of Arjun's words settles heavily over the group, the chilling realization of Shakti's true intentions sinking in. They aren't just fighting to survive—they're fighting to keep their very souls from being enslaved.

"Amon, one of gods, has the power to get a hold on Shakhti before he finishes everything. Despite of being a demon I want peace. I have no hunger of ruling universe, but Shakhti has no intention cleaning his thoughts. So, we have to rush our search of Amon. By this time, He might have sensed our presence and he will be searching for us too", arjun adds.

Moments after Shaurya, Amar and Arjun leave the house.

• • •

"The voice belonged to a demon called Venan, a dark entity that had sensed the vulnerability in Vangeliya's soul after the traumatic events of the tornado. Venan was a creature of ancient origins, feeding on fear and uncertainty, and it saw in Vangeliya an opportunity to manifest its power in the world of the living."

CHAPTER FIVE 2012

On the chilly morning of October 3, 1911, in the small town of Strumica, nestled in what was then the Ottoman Empire, a newborn's cry pierced the air. The modest home of the Surchev family was filled with joy as Vangeliya, their first daughter, was born. The midwife, a seasoned woman with years of experience, swaddled the tiny girl in a soft, handwoven blanket and handed her to her mother, Paraskeva. The baby's small, delicate fingers grasped at the air as her mother cradled her, whispering blessings and hopes for her future.

Vangeliya, or Baba Vanga as she would later be known, grew up in a time of great uncertainty, but her early years were marked by the warmth of family and the simple joys of rural life. As she grew, her curious eyes took in the world around her with wonder. She loved to explore the fields surrounding her home, where wildflowers bloomed in vibrant colors, and the air was thick with the scent of earth and greenery.

From an early age, Vangeliya was known for her quick smile and the light in her eyes. She would often play with the other children in the village, their laughter echoing through the narrow streets as they chased each other, barefoot and carefree. One of her favorite pastimes was visiting her grandmother, who lived just a short walk from her home. Her grandmother would tell her stories of ancient heroes and mystical lands, weaving tales that ignited the young girl's imagination.

Vangeliya was particularly fond of the village's seasonal fairs. These were lively events where the townsfolk would gather to celebrate the harvest, share in communal feasts, and enjoy traditional music and dance. She would twirl in circles with the other girls, her braided hair flying, as the music of the gajda and kaval filled the air. Her laughter was infectious, and her joy was pure.

One summer, her father, Pando, crafted a small wooden doll for her, which quickly became her most cherished possession. She would carry it everywhere, whispering secrets to it and imagining grand adventures where the doll was the heroine, much like the stories her grandmother told. Life, though simple, was full of love, community, and the kind of happiness that only comes from the innocence of childhood.

But life in Strumica, like much of the world, was not without its trials. The years passed, and Vangeliya's world would soon be forever altered. It was a warm day in 1923 when the skies darkened unexpectedly. What began as a gentle breeze soon grew into a fierce, howling wind. The villagers, sensing the danger, hurried to secure their homes and livestock, but nothing could have prepared them for what was coming.

Vangeliya, now 12 years old, had been playing in the fields when the tornado struck. The sky turned an ominous shade of black, and the wind roared with an intensity that rattled the very earth. Before she could find shelter, the tornado descended upon the village, ripping through the fields and homes with terrifying force.

Vangeliya was caught in the storm's grip, lifted off the ground as if she were no more than a leaf in the wind. She was thrown across the landscape, her body battered by debris, her screams lost in the cacophony of the storm. When the tornado finally passed, leaving a trail of devastation in its wake, the villagers searched frantically for the missing girl.

They found her unconscious, her small frame covered in dirt and bruises, her once-bright eyes now closed and lifeless. The doctors could do little; the storm had taken her sight. The vibrant world that Vangeliya once knew was plunged into darkness.

In the years that followed, Vangeliya's life changed irrevocably. Her blindness became both a curse and, as the world would later come to see, a gift. The child who once played so freely in the fields would grow into a woman known for her extraordinary abilities, a woman who, despite the darkness that took her sight, would illuminate the lives of many with her visions and prophecies.

But on that fateful day in 1923, as the villagers gathered around the young girl, they could not have known that the loss of her sight would be the beginning of a remarkable journey, one that would see Vangeliya—Baba Vanga—become a figure of great mystery and reverence.

After the tornado took Vangeliya's sight in 1923, life in Strumica returned to its familiar rhythms, but for the now-blind girl, everything had changed. The vibrant world she once knew had vanished, replaced by a vast, unending darkness. But within that darkness, something else began to stir—a presence that would shape her destiny in ways she could never have imagined.

In the weeks following her recovery, Vangeliya started to experience strange sensations. At first, they were subtle—a faint whispering in the back of her mind, a murmur that she couldn't quite make out. But as time passed, the whispers grew louder, more insistent, until they became a constant presence, like a shadow clinging to her every thought.

The voice belonged to a demon called Venan, a dark entity that had sensed the vulnerability in Vangeliya's soul after the traumatic events of the tornado. Venan was a creature of ancient origins, feeding on fear and uncertainty, and it saw in Vangeliya an opportunity to manifest its power in the world of the living.

Venan began to whisper to her, planting images and visions in her mind—glimpses of the future, fragments of events yet to come. At first, Vangeliya was terrified. She couldn't understand what was happening to her. The visions were vivid and unsettling, filled with scenes of joy and despair, life and death. It was as if she had been given a window into a realm beyond human comprehension.

One day, as Vangeliya sat alone in her family's modest home, the whispers took on a new clarity. Venan showed her the fate of a neighbor's child, a boy who had been missing for several days. Vangeliya saw the boy in her mind's eye, lying in a shallow ditch near the edge of the village, injured but alive. The vision was so vivid, so real, that she felt compelled to tell someone.

Trembling with fear and uncertainty, she told her father, Pando, what she had seen. Though skeptical, Pando decided to investigate. To his shock, he found the boy exactly where Vangeliya had described. The news spread quickly through the village—Vangeliya, the blind girl, had seen the future.

At first, the villagers were wary, unsure of how to react to Vangeliya's newfound abilities. But as more of her visions began to come true, their fear turned to awe. Venan's whispers grew more frequent, and with each new vision, Vangeliya's reputation as a seer began to spread beyond Strumica.

Before long, people from neighboring villages started to visit Vangeliya, seeking answers to their most pressing questions. They came to her with desperate hopes and fears, asking about lost loved ones, crops, illnesses, and even their own fates. Vangeliya, guided by Venan's dark whispers, would close her sightless eyes and speak the words that came to her, often in a trance-like state.

Her prophecies were eerily accurate, and the more she spoke, the more people believed. Some saw her as a holy figure, touched by the divine, while others whispered of dark forces at play. But regardless of their beliefs, the people continued to come, drawn by the promise of knowing what lay ahead.

As Venan's influence over Vangeliya grew, so did her fame. Her small home became a pilgrimage site for those seeking answers. People traveled for days, braving harsh weather and treacherous roads, just for a chance to hear her words. Some left with peace of mind, while others were haunted by the dark truths they had learned.

For Vangeliya, the burden of her gift was immense. The visions were relentless, often leaving her exhausted and tormented. She knew that Venan was no benevolent spirit, but a dark force that thrived on the pain and fear her prophecies could bring. Yet, she could not resist its influence. The demon had become a part of her, and with each passing day, it tightened its grip on her soul.

Despite the darkness that surrounded her, Vangeliya continued to help those who sought her out. Her visions, though often tinged with dread, brought clarity to many, and her reputation as a powerful seer only grew. People began to call her Baba Vanga, a name that would echo through the years as both a blessing and a curse.

In time, Baba Vanga's fame would spread far beyond the borders of Strumica, and she would become known throughout the world as a prophetess of extraordinary abilities. But deep within her, Venan's whispers never ceased, a constant reminder of the dark force that had claimed her sight—and her soul. And so, the blind girl who once danced in the fields of her village became a figure shrouded in mystery, her life forever changed by the demon that whispered the future into her mind.

As the years passed and Baba Vanga's fame grew, the whispers of Venan continued to guide her prophecies, often leaving those who sought her counsel both awed and unsettled. But as time wore on, Vangeliya began to notice something strange. The whispers, once constant and insistent, were becoming less frequent. Venan's presence, which had been a dark companion for so long, was beginning to fade.

It was in the early 1990s, when Baba Vanga was already an elderly woman, that Venan whispered to her for what would be the last time. The message was chilling, filled with the weight of finality. In her mind, Vangeliya saw a vision of the world—vast, spinning, alive with billions of lives—and then, just as suddenly, she saw it cease to exist. There was darkness, and then nothingness, as if the very fabric of existence had unraveled.

Venan's voice, cold and distant, spoke of the year 2012. "The world as you know it will end," the demon whispered. "A great change will come, and nothing will ever be the same. This will be the end of all things, the final chapter in the story of mankind."

The vision shook Vangeliya to her core. Despite the many prophecies she had delivered over the years, this one was different. It carried a sense of inevitability that she could not ignore. For days, she grappled with whether to share this dark revelation with the world. But in the end, she decided that the truth, however frightening, must be known.

In 1996, shortly before her death, Baba Vanga made the prediction public. The news spread quickly, sparking fear and speculation across the globe. People from all walks of life—from villagers in remote regions to leaders of powerful nations—pondered the meaning of her words. Some dismissed it as the ramblings of an old woman, while others took it as a dire warning of the apocalypse.

As the year 2012 approached, the prophecy fueled a wave of anxiety and preparation. Books were written, documentaries were made, and countless theories were proposed about what form the end would take. Would it be a natural disaster? A war? A cosmic event? The uncertainty only heightened the fear.

For Baba Vanga, however, the prediction marked the end of an era. After that final prophecy, she noticed that Venan's whispers had completely ceased. The demon that had guided her visions for decades was gone, leaving her in a profound silence she hadn't experienced since childhood. For the first time in years, her mind was her own, free from the dark influence that had both burdened and empowered her.

Baba Vanga passed away in August 1996, never knowing what would come of her final prophecy. As the world held its breath in anticipation of 2012, some believed that her silence after the prediction was a sign that Venan had completed its purpose, or perhaps that it had been vanquished. Others speculated that the demon had left her because the prophecy was set in motion and needed no further intervention.

When 2012 came and went without the cataclysmic event so many had feared, people were left to interpret the prophecy in their own ways. Some believed that the world had indeed ended, but in a metaphorical sense—a shift in consciousness, a change in global dynamics. Others argued that the prophecy had been misunderstood or misinterpreted, while some simply moved on, relieved that the worst had not come to pass.

But for those who had known Baba Vanga, and for those who still believed in her visions, the mystery of her final prophecy—and the silence that followed—remained a haunting enigma, a reminder of the thin line between fate and free will, between the known and the unknowable.

And so, the story of Vangeliya, the blind girl who became Baba Vanga, ended not with the whispers of a demon, but with the quiet that followed—a silence as deep and unfathomable as the visions she once saw.

#

As Arjun stood on the balcony, the city below lay quiet under the veil of night, but his mind was a storm of vivid memories of Vengaliya. The cool air seemed to pulse with the echoes of a cataclysmic battle from the past. His thoughts drifted to 2012, a year that had brought the Earth to the brink of destruction, marked by a cosmic struggle that he had witnessed firsthand as Venan.

The Earth had been in turmoil, writhing under Beren's dark machinations. The ground was convulsing as tectonic plates shattered, sending shockwaves of devastation across cities. The core temperature of the planet had surged, leading to a chaotic maelstrom of earthquakes and volcanic eruptions. Humanity was engulfed in a frenzy of death and destruction as Beren's malevolent influence swept across the globe.

In the midst of this chaos, a cosmic disturbance heralded the arrival of Amon. With a celestial aura that outshone the sun, Amon descended to Earth. His luminous eyes scanned the ravaged world, taking in the dark clouds and the inferno of destruction wrought by Beren. The sky was a turbulent sea of shadow and flame, reflecting the dire state of the world below.

Beren, a figure of ominous power, stood amidst the devastation. His form was cloaked in shadows, his fiery red eyes gleaming with sadistic pleasure. He drew strength from the anguish of those suffering below, reveling in the chaos he had orchestrated.

Amon and Beren faced each other with the Earth as their battleground. Amon raised his hand, unleashing a brilliant beam of pure energy that cut through the darkness like a blade. Beren responded with a wave of his hand, summoning a swirling vortex of dark matter that absorbed and deflected Amon's attack. The clash of light and shadow was a spectacle of celestial power, a testament to the titanic struggle between creation and destruction.

Amon moved with the grace of a divine dancer, his form shimmering with an ethereal glow. He conjured gusts of wind that roared through the air, each gust carrying a purifying force that pushed back against Beren's dark energies. The elemental struggle painted a stark contrast between the forces of light and the forces of chaos.

Beren, undeterred, called upon the chaotic energy he had unleashed. He conjured fissures in the ground, sending waves of molten lava toward Amon. The lava surged with the intensity of his rage, a manifestation of his desire to consume and obliterate. Amon countered with a shield of light that absorbed the lava, turning it into harmless steam.

The sky became a battleground as Amon wielded bolts of lightning that crackled with divine power, striking Beren with precision. The demon retaliated with dark lightning, its jagged tendrils crackling with malevolent energy. The forces clashed in mid-air, creating explosions of light and shadow that illuminated the night.

Beren's eyes blazed with fury as he summoned monstrous entities from the shadows—horrific creatures that roared with insatiable hunger. Amon responded by calling forth celestial beings of pure light, their forms shining like stars as they battled Beren's minions. The battlefield was alive with the struggle between these supernatural forces, each side fighting for the fate of Earth and the universe.

As the conflict reached its zenith, Amon drew upon his full divine power. He ascended into the sky, his form expanding into a radiant aura that encompassed the planet. With a sweeping gesture, he unleashed a wave of pure, healing energy that washed over the Earth, reversing the damage caused by Beren's cosmic manipulation. The ground began to heal, the earthquakes subsided, and the fires extinguished.

Beren, overwhelmed by Amon's power, struggled to maintain his form. His dark figure flickered and wavered as the divine light pierced through his defenses. In a final, desperate act, Beren attempted a cataclysmic explosion, but Amon countered with a barrier of radiant light that absorbed and neutralized the attack.

Exhausted and defeated, Beren's dark form dissipated into the ether, his influence over the universe receding. The chaos that had consumed the world began to abate, and the celestial forces returned to their natural harmony. Amon, his divine form still glowing softly, descended back to Earth.

As he touched down amidst the recovering planet, he looked upon the world with a sense of solemn satisfaction. The devastation had been averted, and humanity had been given a second chance. Amon chose to remain on Earth, a guardian against future cosmic threats, ensuring that the balance was maintained.

Standing on the balcony, Arjun recalled the epic battle between Amon and his brother Beren, the struggle that had shaped the fate of the world. The echoes of Beren's dark ambitions and Amon's heroic actions were a reminder of the delicate balance between destruction and preservation. As Arjun took a final drag from his cigarette, he let go of the past, focusing on the present. He was no longer merely Venan, but Arjun—a man caught between his turbulent history and the challenges of the present. The weight of his memories and the lessons they carried would guide him as he sought balance in a world that remained ever precarious.

• • •

"Arthur's eyes snapped open, his breath catching in his throat. The name echoed in his mind, resonating with a power that made his skin crawl. He had never heard of Shakhti before, yet he knew, with a certainty that defied logic, that this was no ordinary entity. This was a being of immense power, a supreme demon, whose presence on Earth could only mean one thing: something catastrophic was unfolding, something that defied the boundaries of science and entered the realm of the supernatural."

CHAPTER **SIX** AMON

The presentation room was an impressive space, designed to foster intellectual exchange and cutting-edge discussion. The walls were lined with high-definition screens displaying intricate diagrams and data sets. At the front of the room stood Arthur Brown, a young and brilliant British scientist. His demeanor was confident yet approachable, his voice clear and resonant, reflecting both his deep understanding of the subject and his excitement about the work at hand.

On the main screen behind him, a 3D model of the photon collider's cooling vessel was rotating slowly, highlighting various components as Arthur spoke. The vessel, a massive structure designed to withstand extreme temperatures and pressures, was crucial to the success of the experiment aimed at replicating conditions just after the Big Bang.

"Ladies and gentlemen," Arthur began, addressing the assembly of esteemed scientists from around the world. "As we all know, maintaining the integrity of the collider's vessel during operation is paramount. Any deviation in temperature could lead to catastrophic failures. Over the past few weeks, my team and I have focused on refining the cooling systems, which are vital to ensuring the stability of the vessel."

He pointed to a section of the 3D model where intricate pipelines snaked through the vessel, designed to circulate supercooled liquid helium. "The key challenge," Arthur continued, "has been achieving uniform cooling across the entire structure. After extensive simulations and small-scale tests, we've implemented a new design for the coolant distribution system. This has led to a significant reduction in thermal gradients, thereby minimizing the risk of localized stress and potential fractures."

The room buzzed with interest as Arthur explained the technical details, showing graphs that illustrated the improved temperature consistency. His findings were groundbreaking, pushing the experiment closer to replicating the Big Bang conditions with unprecedented accuracy.

As Arthur concluded his presentation, the room erupted in applause. The moderator, a senior physicist with decades of experience, stepped forward. "Thank you, Arthur, for that enlightening presentation. We'll now open the floor for questions."

A renowned scientist from Japan, known for his expertise in quantum mechanics, raised his hand. "Mr. Brown, could you elaborate on how the new coolant system addresses the issue of micro-cracks forming at the vessel's joints due to thermal stress?"

Arthur nodded, acknowledging the importance of the question. "Certainly. The new system employs a feedback loop that monitors the temperature at critical points in real time. If a thermal spike is detected, the system dynamically adjusts the flow rate of the coolant to that specific area, effectively preventing the formation of micro-cracks. We've tested this extensively, and the results have been very promising."

Another scientist, this time from Germany, asked, "What about the potential for coolant leakage? Have you considered the implications of such an event during full-scale operation?"

Arthur responded with the same calm confidence. "Excellent point. We've reinforced all critical joints with a new alloy composite that is both lightweight and extremely durable. Additionally, the system is designed with multiple redundancies. If a leak is detected, the affected section can be isolated and shut down without compromising the rest of the system."

The discussion continued with more questions from the audience, each answered by Arthur with precision and depth. He demonstrated not only his expertise but also his ability to communicate complex ideas clearly, ensuring that even those outside his immediate field could grasp the significance of his work.

By the end of the session, it was clear that Arthur's contributions had not only advanced the photon collider project but had also earned him the respect and admiration of his peers. The presentation was a resounding success, further cementing his role as a key figure in one of the most ambitious scientific endeavors of the century.

After the successful presentation, Arthur found himself sitting in the canteen with his friends, Sara and Eric. The canteen was bustling with activity, filled with scientists and researchers discussing the day's events over coffee and sandwiches. The trio sat at a small table by the window, where the soft afternoon light filtered through, creating a warm and relaxed atmosphere.

Sara, a brilliant physicist known for her quick wit, raised her cup in a mock toast. "To Arthur, the man of the hour! That presentation was something else. You had the entire room hanging on your every word."

Eric, who specialized in materials science, chimed in, "Yeah, you really knocked it out of the park, mate. I could see the wheels turning in everyone's heads, especially when you talked about the coolant system. It's going to make a huge difference."

Arthur smiled, a mix of pride and relief washing over him. "Thanks, guys. I'm just glad it went well. There was a lot riding on that presentation."

Sara leaned in, her eyes sparkling with excitement. "It's not just that it went well, Arthur. You've really made a name for yourself here. The way you handled those questions was impressive. You're definitely on your way to becoming a key player in this project."

As they continued chatting, the conversation drifted to lighter topics—plans for their upcoming break in the UK, funny anecdotes from past conferences, and the peculiarities of working in different countries. Laughter filled the air as they shared stories, enjoying the rare moments of downtime in their demanding schedules.

Suddenly, in the midst of their conversation, Arthur felt a strange sensation in his chest. It was subtle at first, like a faint flutter, but then it grew stronger, a deep, almost unsettling pressure that seemed to radiate outward. He paused mid-sentence, his hand instinctively moving to his chest.

"Arthur, you, okay?" Eric asked, noticing the change in his friend's expression.

Arthur quickly composed himself, pushing the sensation aside. "Yeah, I'm fine. Just… probably too much coffee," he said with a reassuring smile, though a slight unease lingered in the back of his mind.

Sara looked at him closely, concerned.

"You sure? You've been under a lot of stress lately. Maybe you need to take it easy for a bit."

"I'm good, really," Arthur insisted, taking a deep breath. The sensation had faded, and he didn't want to worry his friends.

"It's just been a long day. Let's not dwell on it."

They continued their conversation, the moment passing as quickly as it had come. But Arthur couldn't shake the feeling entirely. It was as if his body was trying to tell him something, though he wasn't quite sure what.

As the afternoon turned to evening, the three of them decided to head back to their hotel. They had a flight scheduled to the UK later that night, and there were still a few things to wrap up before they leave China.

Walking through the bustling streets of the city, Arthur felt a slight breeze on his face, the cool air calming him. Sara and Eric were chatting animatedly about their plans once they were back in the UK, but Arthur's thoughts kept drifting back to the strange sensation he had felt earlier.

By the time they reached the hotel, the feeling had faded into a distant memory, overshadowed by the excitement of heading home. As they packed up their belongings and prepared for their flight, Arthur pushed the lingering doubts out of his mind, focusing instead on the journey ahead.

The hum of the airplane engines filled the cabin as Arthur, Sara, and Eric settled into their seats. The flight to the UK had taken off smoothly, and the cabin lights were dimmed to a soft, calming glow. Most of the passengers were either sleeping or quietly engrossed in their own thoughts. Eric had already drifted off, his head resting against the window, while Sara was flipping through a magazine, her face relaxed after the long day.

Arthur, however, was far from relaxed. He stared out the window, but his mind was a thousand miles away. The strange sensation he had felt earlier in the day refused to leave him. It was no longer just a fleeting discomfort; it was a gnawing unease that had settled deep within him. He couldn't shake the feeling that something far beyond his understanding was at play.

As he stared into the darkness outside, the faint reflections of the cabin lights on the window seemed to blur and twist, as if reality itself was bending around him. He closed his eyes, hoping to calm his racing thoughts, but instead, he was drawn deeper into the feeling that had haunted him since the canteen.

Suddenly, an image flashed in his mind—an overwhelming presence, dark and powerful, like a shadow that consumed everything in its path. It wasn't just a feeling; it was a force, ancient and malevolent, that seemed to reach across time and space. The name came to him unbidden, as though it had always been there, lurking in the recesses of his mind.

Shakhti.

Arthur's eyes snapped open, his breath catching in his throat. The name echoed in his mind, resonating with a power that made his skin crawl. He had never heard of Shakhti before, yet he knew, with a certainty that defied logic, that this was no ordinary entity. This was a being of immense power, a supreme demon, whose presence on Earth could only mean one thing: something catastrophic was unfolding, something that defied the boundaries of science and entered the realm of the supernatural.

The unease he had felt earlier wasn't just stress or exhaustion; it was his spiritual senses, heightened beyond anything he had ever experienced, reacting to the proximity of a celestial force. It was as though his very soul had recognized the danger long before his conscious mind had caught up.

"Arthur?" Sara's voice broke through his thoughts, soft and concerned.

He turned to her, trying to mask the turmoil raging inside him. "Yeah?"

"You seem really out of it. Are you sure you're, okay?" she asked, her brow furrowed as she looked at him with genuine concern.

Arthur hesitated, not wanting to alarm her. "Just… a lot on my mind," he said, forcing a smile. "The presentation, the project… everything."

Sara nodded, but her eyes didn't leave his. "Well, if you need to talk about anything, we're here. Don't try to take it all on yourself."

"Thanks, Sara," he replied, appreciating her support more than she knew. But this was something he couldn't explain to her—not yet, not when he himself was struggling to understand it.

As the plane soared through the night sky, Arthur felt the weight of the knowledge he now carried pressing down on him. Shakhti was on Earth, and whatever this demon's purpose was, it was far beyond the realm of the scientific experiments they were conducting. It was something otherworldly, something that could change the course of human history.

He glanced at Eric, who was still sleeping soundly, and then back at Sara, who had returned to her magazine but was still glancing at him out of the corner of her eye. They were his friends, his colleagues, and they trusted him. But how could he protect them from something so far beyond their comprehension? How could he even begin to explain what he was sensing?

As the flight continued, Arthur's thoughts churned, a storm of uncertainty and fear. He knew that whatever was coming, it was only the beginning. And somehow, he was at the center of it all.

The plane touched down in the UK just as dawn was breaking, casting a soft glow over the runway. Arthur, Sara, and Eric collected their bags and made their way through the terminal, exhausted but relieved to be back on home soil. As they stepped outside, the crisp morning air reminded them they were far from the warmer climes of China.

A cab driver was waiting for them, holding a sign with Arthur's name on it. He was a middle-aged man with a friendly smile and a distinct Cockney accent. "Morning, folks. Need a lift?"

The three exchanged tired smiles and nodded, grateful for the ride. They loaded their bags into the boot, and soon they were settled in the backseat, the cab pulling away from the curb and merging into the early morning traffic.

The streets of London were just beginning to stir, with only a few cars on the road. As the cab weaved through the city, Sara and Eric began chatting about their trip to China.

"Can you believe that hotpot place in Beijing?" Eric said with a chuckle. "It was out of this world!"

Sara laughed, nodding in agreement. "And the night market! I've never seen anything like it. I'm still trying to wrap my head around the fact that we ate fried scorpions."

Eric grimaced playfully. "You've got stronger guts than me, Sara. I'm sticking to fish and chips from now on."

Their conversation continued, filled with lighthearted banter and shared memories of their time abroad. But Arthur, sitting quietly by the window, was lost in his own thoughts. The unsettling sensation he'd felt on the plane, and the name *Shakhti* that had echoed in his mind, lingered like a dark cloud over him. He couldn't shake the feeling that something ominous was brewing.

As the cab approached Sara's neighborhood, Arthur tried to focus on the conversation, but his mind kept drifting back to that sense of impending danger.

"Arthur, you're awfully quiet," Sara said, turning to him as they neared her stop. "You sure you're alright?"

Arthur forced a smile, trying to push aside his worries. "Yeah, just knackered, I suppose."

The cab came to a stop outside Sara's flat, and she gathered her things. "Right, this is me. See you two later!"

"Take care," Eric said with a wave.

"Get some rest, Sara," Arthur added, his voice sincere but still distant.

Sara stepped out of the cab, waving as she crossed the road. It was a quiet street, with only a few cars moving along, the city still waking up.

But then, something caught Arthur's attention. A bus at the far end of the street was hurtling towards Sara, swerving uncontrollably as it crashed into parked cars on the roadside. Arthur's eyes widened in horror as he realized the bus's brakes had failed.

"Sara, watch out!" he shouted, but she was already in the middle of the road, frozen in panic as the bus sped toward her.

Time seemed to slow as adrenaline surged through Arthur's body. He flung the car door open and bolted towards Sara, moving faster than he had ever thought possible. His legs pumped like pistons, carrying him across the distance in an instant. Just as the bus was about to reach her, Arthur grabbed Sara and yanked her out of the way, rolling them both onto the pavement just as the bus thundered past.

Sara was trembling, her eyes wide with shock. "Arthur… you saved me. I—I couldn't move…"

Arthur helped her sit up, his heart pounding. "It's alright. You're safe now," he said, trying to calm her. But as he looked up, he saw the bus still careening down the street, heading towards a busy intersection.

"I need to stop it," Arthur muttered, determination filling his voice.

Before Sara could respond, Arthur was already on his feet, sprinting after the bus. His movements were a blur, faster than any normal person could possibly achieve. He overtook cars as if they were standing still, his mind focused entirely on the out-of-control vehicle ahead.

As he reached the bus, he leaped onto the back, pulling himself up and smashing through the emergency exit. Inside, the passengers were screaming in terror as the driver frantically tried to brake, his face pale with fear.

"It's not stopping!" the driver yelled, his hands white-knuckled on the wheel.

Arthur grabbed the driver's arm. "Give it another go," he commanded, his voice steady.

The driver hit the brakes with all his might, and this time, Arthur focused, feeling a surge of energy welling up from deep within him. He channeled his supernatural abilities. The bus shuddered violently as if resisting his power, but Arthur held firm, his will unwavering. With a screech of metal and a jolt that shook the entire vehicle, the bus finally came to a halt, mere feet from the crowded intersection. The passengers were thrown forward but safe, their cries of panic turning to gasps of relief.

They began to applaud, some of them in tears, thanking Arthur for saving their lives. The driver looked at him in disbelief. "How...?"

Arthur simply nodded, not offering an explanation. He quickly exited the bus and ran back down the street to where he had left Sara.

She was still sitting on the pavement, her hands trembling as she tried to steady her breathing. Eric joined her while she was sitting. When Arthur reached her, he knelt down beside her, his expression softening.

"Sara, are you alright?" he asked gently.

She looked up at him, her eyes filled with gratitude and confusion. "Arthur… that bus… it should've hit me. But you… and then you ran so fast… How did you do that?"

Arthur hesitated, unsure of how much to reveal. "I don't know, Sara. I just… reacted."

She nodded, still shaken but beginning to calm down. "Thank you. You saved my life."

He offered her a hand, helping her to her feet. "Let's get you home."

They walked together in silence, the events of the last few minutes hanging heavily between them. When they reached Sara's front door, Arthur and Eric made sure she was steady on her feet before letting go.

"Are you sure you're, okay?" he asked, his concern evident.

Sara nodded, though her expression was still filled with uncertainty. "Yeah, I'll be fine. I just… need to process everything."

"Take your time," Arthur said softly. "And if you need anything, ring me, alright?"

She smiled weakly. "I will. Thanks, Arthur."

As Sara walked inside, both watched her go, a mix of emotions churning within him. He knew that whatever had happened today was just the beginning. The power he had used to stop the bus was not something he fully understood, but it was a stark reminder of the truth he had kept hidden for so long—the truth about who he really was.

Arthur Brown was just a name, a persona he had crafted to blend into the world of mortals. But deep down, he was not an ordinary man. He was *Amon*, a god whose presence on Earth was meant to remain a secret. For centuries, he had walked among humans, disguising his true nature, living quietly, and avoiding the use of his powers unless absolutely necessary.

Today, however, had been different. The threat to Sara's life had triggered something deep within him, forcing him to reveal a glimpse of his divine abilities. The connection to *Shakhti*, the supreme demon, had only heightened his awareness that his past was catching up to him.

Aurther dropped Eric and returned his home. As he turned and began the walk to his own home, Arthur's mind was filled with questions and the looming realization that the time for hiding might soon come to an end. He had sworn to protect the world from the forces that sought to disrupt it, but doing so without revealing his true identity was becoming increasingly difficult. For now, he would continue to play the role of Arthur Brown, the scientist, the friend. But deep inside, Amon, the god, remained vigilant, knowing that the battle against Shakhti and the secrets of his own past were just beginning.

• • •

"But then, as quickly as the transformation occurred, it reverses. Khan's intimidating figure fades, and Arjun reappears, his expression now serious and determined. Jay and Amar exchange a look, still processing what they've just witnessed."

CHAPTER
SEVEN LANKA

Morning sunlight filters through the curtains, casting a warm glow across the living room where Amar and Arjun are seated on a worn-out couch. The room is still, but there's an undercurrent of tension in the air. Amar, with his brows furrowed, flips through a stack of documents, while Arjun absently sips his tea, his eyes distant as if lost in thought.

Suddenly, the silence is shattered by the sharp sound of the doorbell ringing insistently. Amar's head snaps up, and he exchanges a quick, concerned glance with Arjun. Without a word, he springs to his feet and rushes to the door. He swings it open to reveal Jay, standing there with a look of panic etched across his face, beads of sweat glistening on his forehead despite the cool morning air.

Before Amar can speak, Jay pushes past him, entering the room with a sense of urgency. "I've got intel regarding Javed Ustad," he blurts out, his voice tinged with anxiety. "We have to rush to arrest him now. If we can get to him, we might unravel their entire plan."

Amar closes the door behind Jay, his face growing more serious. "Where is he now?" Arjun asks, his voice steady but with an edge that suggests he's already mentally preparing for action.

Jay turns to face Arjun, his eyes wide with the weight of his news. "Sri Lanka! One of Javed's men spilled the location. I don't have all the details, but I suspect something big is being planned there. If Javed knows about Khan, he'll be speeding things up."

Arjun nods, absorbing the information as Amar moves to the wall where a calendar hangs, its pages marked with notes and dates. "Yes, and if he's aware of Khan, we're running out of time." Amar runs a hand through his hair, his eyes fixating on a specific date. "Independence Day is only 10 days away. If Javed's planning something for then, we're sitting on a ticking time bomb. The city is just starting to calm down after what happened last week. If something goes wrong on Independence Day..."

Amar trails off, his mind racing through scenarios, each more dire than the last. Jay, sensing the gravity of the situation, steps forward. "We need a plan," he says, his voice steady, but there's a crack in his composure, a flicker of fear that only those closest to him would notice.

Amar, still staring at the calendar, slowly turns back to face Jay and Arjun. But as he does, he freezes, his eyes widening in disbelief. Arjun is no longer the man who sat sipping tea just moments ago. He transforms himself into Khan, his smirk cold and calculating, his presence almost suffocating in its intensity.

Khan takes a step forward, his voice dripping with confidence. "I guess I have a better plan," he says, his eyes gleaming with a dangerous light. The room, filled with the warmth of the morning sun, now feels cold and menacing.

But then, as quickly as the transformation occurred, it reverses. Khan's intimidating figure fades, and Arjun reappears, his expression now serious and determined. Jay and Amar exchange a look, still processing what they've just witnessed.

Arjun takes a deep breath, his voice steady but laced with urgency. "I can infiltrate Javed's men," he says, locking eyes with Amar and Jay. "As Khan, I can get close to him, find out what he's planning. He doesn't know who I really am—this could be our best chance to stop whatever he's got in store."

Jay looks at Arjun, the tension in his posture easing slightly as the plan takes shape in his mind. "You're risking a lot, Arjun. If Javed suspects anything..."

Arjun cuts him off, his resolve unshakable. "It's a risk I'm willing to take. We don't have time for anything else. If we can figure out his intentions before Independence Day, we can stop him and keep the city safe."

Amar nods, the pieces of the plan falling into place. "Alright," he says, his voice firm. "We'll support you from here, gather whatever intel we can, and stay ready for your signal. But remember, you're not alone in this."

Arjun offers a small, reassuring smile. "I know. But if this works, it'll give us the upper hand."

The room settles into a focused silence, the earlier tension replaced with a shared sense of purpose. The next few days would be critical, but with Arjun's ability to slip into the role of Khan, they now had a fighting chance to stop Javed and protect the city from whatever he had planned.

#

The air is thick with humidity as Arjun approaches the heavily guarded entrance of Javed Ustad's hidden base. The compound is nestled deep within the Sri Lankan jungle, concealed from prying eyes by a labyrinth of trees and foliage. His heart pounds beneath his calm exterior, but Arjun knows what he must do. In a hidden spot just outside the compound, he pauses, taking a deep breath.

Closing his eyes, Arjun taps into the power within him, feeling the familiar energy coursing through his veins. Slowly, his appearance begins to shift—the contours of his face sharpen, his posture changes, becoming more imposing, and his eyes take on a colder, more calculating gleam. His entire aura transforms, the warm and approachable Arjun disappearing, replaced by the dangerous and fearsome Khan.

When he opens his eyes, the transformation is complete. Khan stands where Arjun once was, exuding an air of authority and menace. Confident in his disguise, Khan strides toward the compound's entrance. The guards—hardened men with cold, suspicious eyes—glance at him but then immediately lower their weapons, recognizing the infamous figure before them. Whispers ripple through the ranks as they realize who has come to visit.

Inside the base, Javed Ustad sits in a grand room adorned with rich, dark wood and tapestries that tell the stories of battles long past. He is a grizzled man, with sharp features and eyes that gleam with malice. As the door swings open and Khan steps in, Javed's eyes light up with a mix of surprise and delight. He rises from his seat, his movements slow but filled with an underlying strength.

"Khan!" Javed exclaims, his voice resonating with both joy and disbelief. "*Ae malik kitani meherbaniyan karega tu*.....I thought you were dead! The rumors said you had vanished."

Khan lets out a low, confident chuckle as he steps forward. "Rumors are a poor man's truth. It takes more than whispers to kill me."

Javed approaches Khan, clasping his shoulders in a gesture of camaraderie. "It's good to see you, old friend. You've been missed. Come, sit with me. We must celebrate your return with a *dawat*!"

With a wave of his hand, Javed orders his men to prepare a feast. The room is soon bustling with activity as tables are laid with rich foods and drinks. Khan takes his place beside Javed at the head of the table, careful to maintain his confident, almost arrogant demeanor.

As the evening progresses, Javed grows more relaxed, his initial wariness fading in the presence of someone he believes to be a trusted ally. Khan uses this to his advantage, steering the conversation toward the future, toward Javed's plans.

"You've always been a man with grand designs, Javed," Khan says smoothly, taking a sip of his drink. "But the world has changed. The authorities are tightening their grip. What's your next move?"

Javed leans back in his chair, a dark smile playing on his lips. The alcohol has loosened his tongue, and the presence of Khan, whom he considers a kindred spirit, makes him more willing to boast. "Khan, my friend, you know me too well. I've been quiet for a while, but not idle."

He lowers his voice, leaning closer to Khan, as if sharing a prized secret. "I have something big planned. A gift to our enemies, a reminder of our strength. 300 kilograms of RDX, Khan, enough to make the world tremble. It's already on its way to India."

Khan's heart skips a beat, but he maintains his composure, his expression unreadable. "RDX?" he repeats, feigning casual interest. "That's a lot of firepower. What do you plan to do with it?"

Javed's eyes gleam with dark satisfaction. "Independence Day is coming up. What better day to strike at the heart of our enemies? I've arranged for coordinated blasts in seven major cities. By the time the sun sets on Independence Day, they'll remember who truly holds the power."

Khan nods slowly, his mind racing as he processes the gravity of the information. "Bold, as always," he says, his voice steady. "But what about security? The cities will be on high alert."

Javed waves a dismissive hand. "I've got it covered. My men are in place, and we've been careful. The bombs will be hidden where they least expect it—inside government buildings, near monuments, where the crowds gather. By the time they realize what's happening, it'll be too late."

Khan forces a smile, raising his glass to Javed. "To victory, then," he says, clinking his glass against Javed's. But behind the facade, his mind is already formulating a plan to relay this critical information back to Amar and Jay.

The *dawat* continues late into the night, but Khan remains vigilant, every word, every gesture calculated to keep Javed convinced that he is back on his side. As the night draws to a close, Javed, satisfied and a little drunk, finally dismisses the gathering.

"Rest here tonight, Khan," Javed says as he stands. "We'll talk more in the morning. There's much to do."

Khan nods, watching as Javed leaves the room, his mind still whirring with the details of the conversation. He knows now that the stakes are even higher than they had imagined. Independence Day is just around the corner, and the clock is ticking.

As Khan is led to a guest room, he mentally prepares himself for the next phase of the plan. He has the information he came for—but getting out of Javed's base alive and passing that information on will be a challenge of its own.

But Khan is no ordinary man. As he closes the door behind him, he allows himself a moment to breathe, the weight of his dual identity heavy on his shoulders.

He's come this far, and he knows he won't stop until Javed's plan is dismantled, and the cities of India are safe.

#

The moonlight seeps through the small window of the guest room where Arjun, still in the form of Khan, sits in deep thought. The information he's just uncovered weighs heavily on him, and he knows time is of the essence. With the compound quiet and Javed's men asleep, it's the perfect moment to act.

Arjun rises from the bed and takes a deep breath, feeling the familiar energy coursing through his body. He focuses, his form beginning to shift once more. The sharp features of Khan soften, his stature reduces, and his expression becomes more earnest. Within moments, Arjun has returned to his true self.

Glancing around the dimly lit room one last time to ensure he's alone, Arjun closes his eyes and concentrates. The energy within him intensifies, and in an instant, he vanishes from the room, leaving behind only the faintest ripple in the air.

In a secure, dimly lit room in Mumbai, Amar and Jay are huddled over a map of the city, discussing possible scenarios and plans of action. The tension is palpable, both men acutely aware of the dangers lurking just days away.

Suddenly, a faint hum fills the air, and before they can react, Arjun materializes in the center of the room. Startled, both men jump to their feet, but their shock quickly turns to relief when they see who it is.

"Arjun!" Amar exclaims, rushing over. "What did you find out?"

Arjun wastes no time, his voice steady but urgent. "Javed has 300 kilograms of RDX. He's planning to use it to carry out coordinated bombings in seven major cities on Independence Day. The explosives are already enroute to India."

Jay's face pales, and Amar's expression hardens. "We need to alert the authorities, get every city on high alert," Amar says, already moving toward a communication device.

Arjun nods, but his voice remains calm as he adds, "Do that, but stay discreet. We can't let Javed or his men catch wind of this. I've earned his trust as Khan, but if he suspects anything, it could all fall apart."

Amar pauses, turning back to Arjun. "What will you do?"

Arjun's eyes are resolute. "I'll go back. I need to gather more details—where the RDX is hidden, who his contacts are, how we can intercept it before it's too late. I'll return as Khan and keep them talking."

Jay, still reeling from the gravity of the situation, speaks up. "That's dangerous, Arjun. If anything goes wrong..."

Arjun places a reassuring hand on Jay's shoulder. "I know the risks, but this is the only way. Trust me, I'll be back with the information we need."

Amar nods, his expression one of determination mixed with concern. "We trust you, Arjun. Just be careful."

Arjun smiles briefly, then steps back, once again focusing his energy. With a sharp inhale, he disappears from the safehouse, the room falling silent in his absence.

Back in the guest room where he had been staying, the air stirs as Arjun reappears, the transition smooth and silent. The room is exactly as he left it, the night outside still and quiet. Wasting no time, he concentrates once more, feeling the familiar surge of power as his form begins to shift again.

The warm, earnest features of Arjun give way to the cold, calculating visage of Khan. His posture straightens, his expression hardens, and within seconds, Khan stands in the room, ready to continue his deception.

With a final glance around to ensure everything is in place, Khan smirks to himself. The game is far from over, and now, with the knowledge he's gained, the odds are starting to shift in his favor.

He moves to the door, knowing that by morning, he will once again be face-to-face with Javed Ustad, continuing the dangerous dance that could determine the fate of millions.

The first rays of sunlight pierce through the dense jungle canopy, casting a golden glow over Javed Ustad's hidden base. The compound is already bustling with activity, but deep within its confines, in a private chamber, Javed sits at a table, enjoying his morning tea. Across from him, Khan—who is really Arjun in disguise—sits silently, his eyes sharp, listening intently to every word Javed speaks.

Javed leans back in his chair, a satisfied smile playing on his lips. "The plan is moving smoothly, Khan. The RDX has already been delivered to India. My men have spread it across the locations where the bombs will be assembled."

Arjun, as Khan, nods, his expression unreadable. "Good to hear, Javed. But I'm curious—how are you managing the logistics? Moving that much RDX without attracting attention is no small feat."

Javed chuckles, clearly pleased with himself. "Of course, it isn't. But I've ensured that everything is handled by my most trusted men. The RDX has been divided into smaller packets, spread across the cities where the attacks will take place. It's foolproof."

Arjun, maintaining his calm exterior, presses further. "And where exactly are these packets now? I assume they're being well-guarded."

Javed narrows his eyes slightly, a flicker of suspicion crossing his face. "Why do you ask, Khan? You've never been one for details."

Arjun smiles, his tone casual. "Just making sure we're covered. If anything goes wrong, I need to know where to go to ensure things get back on track."

Javed seemed to relax at this, but suspicion deepened as he knew Khan was a part of plan, Javed gave wrong details as, "Of course. The RDX has been split into three major packets, each containing 100 kilograms. They've been sent to Pune, Ahmadabad, and Patna. From there, my men will divide them further into seven smaller packets, ready to be deployed on Independence Day."

Khan nods, his mind racing as he processes the information. He knows this is the crucial detail they needed, but now he has to figure out how to extract more without raising alarms.

He leans back, pretending to consider Javed's words, for much details Arjun planned something, "Interesting. But Javed, with all the heat on us, don't you think it would be wise to move the location of the final assembly to somewhere… quieter?"

Javed frowns slightly. "What do you mean?"

Khan shrugs, casually gesturing to the guards and other personnel moving around the compound. "Too many eyes here. I'm just saying, if we want to ensure absolute secrecy, maybe we should discuss the final steps somewhere less… populated."

Javed thinks for a moment, then nods. "You may be right, Khan. Let's take a walk."

Javed leads Khan to a more isolated part of the compound, away from the prying eyes and ears of his men. The jungle around them grows denser, the sounds of the base fading into the background as they move deeper into the trees.

Once they reach a secluded spot, Javed turns to Khan, his expression serious. "Alright, we're alone now. What's on your mind?"

Khan's demeanor changes subtly, the cold calculation in his eyes intensifying. "Javed, we've known each other a long time, haven't we? I'm only looking out for our best interests. But there's one more thing I need to know..."

Before Javed can react, Khan strikes, his hand clamping down on Javed's wrist with bone-crushing force. The sudden attack catches Javed off guard, and he stumbles back, fear flashing in his eyes.

"What—what are you doing, Khan?" Javed gasps, struggling against Khan's grip.

Khan, his voice low and dangerous, leans in close. "I'm not Khan, Javed. The real Khan is gone. And now, you're going to tell me exactly where the RDX packets are being split."

Javed's eyes widen in shock, the realization dawning on him too late. He tries to break free, but Arjun is too strong, his grip unyielding. "You... you're one of them! A spy!"

Khan smirks, but there's no humor in it. "Call me whatever you want, but you're going to talk. Now, where are the packets being split?"

Javed struggles, but Khan's strength is overwhelming. After minutes of fruitless resistance, Javed finally breaks, the fear of torture overcoming his loyalty to his cause.

"Alright! Alright, I'll tell you!" Javed gasps, his voice trembling. "The RDX is split into three parts—100 kilograms each. They're being sent to Delhi, Mumbai, and Chennai. That's all I know, I swear!"

Khan tightens his grip for a moment, then abruptly releases Javed, sending him stumbling to the ground. "Thank you, Javed. That's all I needed."

As Javed clutches his wrist in pain, Khan steps back, his expression cold. "Your plan ends here, Javed. India will never bow to the likes of you."

Khan grips Javed on his neck and turned his face to him, He glared inside the eyes and erased recent moments from his head. Javed went unconscious.

Khan vanishes into thin air, leaving him alone in the jungle, bewildered and defeated.

Amar and Jay are in the midst of coordinating their response when Arjun materializes in the room, his expression grim. The urgency in his demeanor immediately catches their attention.

"Arjun!" Amar exclaims. "What happened?"

Arjun wastes no time. "I got the information we needed. The RDX is split into three parts, 100 kilograms each, and they're already in India—Delhi, Mumbai, and Chennai. From there, they'll be divided into seven smaller packets for the attacks."

Jay looks horrified. "We need to stop them, now."

Amar nods, already moving to make the necessary calls. "We'll alert the authorities in all three cities. We need to track down those packets before they can be deployed."

Arjun places a reassuring hand on Amar's shoulder. "Do what you need to do. I'm going back to make sure Javed and his men don't change the plan or try to move the RDX again."

Before Amar or Jay can respond, Arjun closes his eyes, focusing his energy. In an instant, he disappears from the safehouse, leaving them to carry out the next phase of the plan.

Inside the room where Arjun had been staying as Khan, the air ripples as he reappears, his form already shifting back into the guise of Khan. Within seconds, the transformation is complete, and Khan stands once again in the room, his expression steely and determined.

Javed who was brought back in his room by one of his men as he found him unconscious. Khan entered Javed's room and convinces him walk with him again to the rear of the hideout in jungle.

Javed secretly signals some of his main to keep watch on both of them while agreed to walk with khan. He smirks to himself as he steps out of the room.

As they approach a dense thicket of trees, Khan suddenly stops. Javed, sensing something amiss, turns to face him, confusion flickering across his face.

"Why have we stopped?" Javed asks, his voice tinged with suspicion.

Khan smirks, his eyes narrowing. "Because, Javed, it's time you knew the truth."

Before Javed can react, Khan's form begins to shimmer and shift. His tall, imposing figure morphs, shrinking and reshaping until Arjun stands before him, his true form revealed. The look of shock and fear on Javed's face is instantaneous.

"You… you're not Khan," Javed stammers, taking a step back.

"No," Arjun replies coldly. "Khan is dead. And soon, so will you be."

Without warning, Arjun lunges forward, grabbing Javed by the collar and lifting him effortlessly off the ground. With a swift motion, he hurls Javed into a nearby tree. The impact forces the air from Javed's lungs, and before he can catch his breath, Arjun waves his hand, his powers flaring.

The tree begins to warp and twist around Javed, its bark and wood creeping up his body, fusing him to its trunk. Javed struggles, terror overtaking him as the wood climbs higher, but his efforts are futile.

Arjun steps closer, his voice calm but laced with menace. "Khan is gone, Javed. And your reign of terror ends now. Soon, this entire base, along with you, will be reduced to ashes."

Javed's eyes widen in horror as the wood encases him up to his neck, his head left exposed. He can feel the life being drained from him, the tree consuming him slowly, painfully. He tries to plead, but Arjun has already turned away.

Arjun walks back toward the base, leaving Javed half-fused with the tree, his screams of agony echoing through the jungle. The base comes into view, and Arjun knows what must be done. The time for mercy has passed

As Arjun approaches the base, Javed's men, unaware of what has just transpired, move to intercept him. But Arjun's resolve is unshakable. With a single gesture, he eliminates them, their bodies crumpling to the ground as he passes through the base unchallenged.

Reaching the heart of the base, Arjun picks up a match from a nearby table. He ignites it, watching the small flame dance for a moment before flicking it into the dry foliage surrounding the base. The fire catches quickly, but this is only the beginning.

Arjun raises his hands, summoning the full extent of his power. The flames grow and twist, swirling around him as he manipulates the fire with ease. A tornado of fire erupts from the ground, its fiery tendrils reaching up into the sky, roaring with fury. The inferno consumes everything in its path—buildings, equipment, and the bodies of Javed's men, all reduced to ash in moments.

The fire tornado tears through the base, unstoppable, until it reaches the tree where Javed is trapped. His final screams are drowned out by the roar of the flames as the fire engulfs him, leaving nothing behind but scorched earth.

Arjun stands at the center of the destruction, watching as the base is obliterated, ensuring that no trace of Javed's plans or men remains. Satisfied that the job is done, he allows the fire to die down, the flames retreating back into the earth.

Without a word, Arjun disappears, his form vanishing from the smoldering ruins.

Arjun reappears in the safehouse, his presence immediately felt by Amar and Jay, who turn to him with expectant expressions.

"It's done," Arjun says simply. "Javed and his base are no more. The RDX plans are ruined. Now we just need to clean up the remnants in India."

Amar nods, relief washing over him. "We'll handle it. You've done more than enough, Arjun."

Jay smiles, though there's a trace of concern in his eyes. "What about you? You've been through a lot."

Arjun shakes his head, his expression resolute. "I'm fine. We still have work to do. But for now, the worst is over."

With the immediate threat neutralized, Arjun allows himself a moment of rest, knowing that while the battle is won, the war against those like Javed is far from over.

The room is filled with a tense but relieved silence as Arjun, Amar, and Jay reflects on the events of the past few hours. The destruction of Javed's base has lifted a heavy weight from their shoulders, but the air is still thick with the anticipation of what comes next.

Arjun, standing near the window, gazes out at the first light of dawn creeping over the city. A faint smile plays on his lips, but there's a tightness in his expression that neither Amar nor Jay notices—at first.

Suddenly, Arjun winces, his hand instinctively clutching his side. The discomfort he's been ignoring intensifies, spreading through his body like wildfire. His breathing becomes labored, each breath more difficult than the last.

Amar, noticing Arjun's sudden change in demeanor, takes a step toward him. "Arjun? Are you okay?"

Before Arjun can respond, the pain hits him full force. It's as if his body is being torn apart from the inside, the unbearable agony making it impossible to stand. He doubles over, clutching his chest, his vision blurring as he tries to fight the pain.

Jay, now alarmed, rushes to his side. "Arjun! What's happening?"

Arjun grits his teeth, struggling to stay on his feet. But the pain is too much. His powers, which have always been under his control, now feel like they're spiraling out of reach. He tries to speak, to reassure them, but all that comes out is a strangled gasp.

"Arjun, talk to us!" Amar demands, his voice filled with worry.

But before they can do anything, Arjun's body begins to flicker, his form destabilizing as if he's caught between two worlds. The sensation is unlike anything he's ever felt, a wrenching pull that seems to be dragging him away. With a final, agonized cry, Arjun disappears from the room, leaving Amar and Jay in stunned silence. The space where he stood is now empty, the air thick with the tension of his sudden, inexplicable departure.

Amar and Jay exchange a shocked look, the reality of what just happened slowly sinking in.

"What... what just happened?" Jay whispers, his voice shaking with confusion and fear.

"I don't know," Amar replies, his face pale. "But whatever it was, it wasn't good."

The two men stand frozen in place, the weight of the unknown pressing down on them. Their friend and ally are gone, and they have no idea where—or what—has taken him.

•••

"Shakhti's eyes blaze with fury, but there's a hint of something else—fear. He channels all his energy into a desperate counterattack, summoning a massive wave of dark energy that surges toward Beren like a tidal wave. But Beren meets it head-on, his obsidian claws slicing through the energy as if it were nothing more than mist."

CHAPTER **EIGHT** REUNION

Arjun, still reeling from the intense pain that ripped through him, finds himself engulfed in darkness. The air is thick, heavy with the stench of decay and the echoing cries of tormented souls. He tries to steady himself, but the ground beneath his feet feels unstable, as if it's shifting under his weight. The darkness is not just an absence of light; it's a living, breathing entity that seems to press in on him from all sides.

As his vision adjusts, Arjun realizes he's no longer in the safehouse. He's been transported to a place far more sinister—the Dark World, a realm of demons and forgotten gods, where the very fabric of reality bends to the will of those who control it.

The landscape is a twisted version of a world he once knew. Jagged mountains loom in the distance, their peaks obscured by swirling black clouds. Rivers of molten lava cut through the charred earth, casting an eerie, red glow that flickers like the dying embers of a fire. The sky above is a churning mass of shadows, with no stars or moon to break the oppressive gloom.

Arjun knows this place all too well. It's a realm he's visited in his darkest moments, where he's battled the demons that dwell within him. But this time, something feels different—more dangerous, more real.

Suddenly, the ground trembles beneath him, and a deep, resonant voice fills the air, echoing from every direction.

"Welcome home, my son."

Arjun stiffens, his heart pounding in his chest. He knows that voice—the voice of his father, Shakhti, the supreme demon. The one he's fought against all his life, the one he's tried to distance himself from, to deny the demonic heritage that runs through his veins.

Out of the shadows, a figure emerges, towering and imposing. Shakhti is a monstrous being, his form shifting and warping with every step he takes. His skin is a deep, unnatural red, covered in dark, pulsating veins that seem to throb with malevolent energy. His eyes are pits of darkness, devoid of any humanity, and his mouth curls into a cruel, twisted smile, revealing rows of sharp, blackened teeth.

He's dressed in a cloak made from the skins of fallen warriors; their faces still etched in eternal agony. In his hand, he wields a massive, obsidian staff, its surface covered in ancient runes that glow with a sickly green light.

Arjun tries to summon his strength, but the pain that brought him here still lingers, weakening him. He stands his ground, glaring at Shakhti with defiance.

"What do you want?" Arjun spits, his voice filled with venom. "I didn't come here willingly."

Shakhti chuckles, a low, rumbling sound that reverberates through the very earth beneath them. "Oh, but you did, Venan. You cannot deny your true nature forever. The power within you—the power I gave you—has brought you here. It's time you accepted who you really are."

Arjun clenches his fists, the anger within him building. "I'm nothing like you. I've spent my life fighting against the darkness you've tried to force on me."

"Is that so?" Shakhti's voice is mocking, dripping with disdain. "You may fight it, but you cannot escape it. You are my creation, Venan. The darkness is in you, whether you want to admit it or not."

He takes a step closer, his massive form looming over Arjun. "Join me, my son. Surrender to your true self, and together, we will destroy the gods who have oppressed us for eons. We will rule the mortal and immortal realms alike. The power we could wield together is beyond your imagination."

Arjun's eyes narrow, his resolve hardening. "I'll never join you. I'll never become what you are."

Shakhti's smile fades, replaced by a scowl of frustration. "You're a fool, Venan. You've seen the power you possess—the power that comes from me. Do you really think you can stand against the gods alone? With me by your side, we could be unstoppable!"

Arjun shakes his head, taking a step back. "I'd rather die fighting than live as a monster under your rule."

Shakhti's eyes flare with anger, and the ground beneath them cracks and shatters, sending shockwaves through the landscape. "So be it, then. If you will not join me willingly, I will make you submit!"

Arjun feels the air around him grow heavy, the pressure almost suffocating. His heart races as he realizes what's coming. He knows he cannot fight Shakhti.

With a deep breath, Arjun summons the darkness within him, the power he's fought to control for so long. body begins to shift, his muscles bulging and twisting as he transforms into his demonic form—Venan.

Venan is a fearsome sight to behold. His skin turns a deep, midnight black, covered in intricate, glowing red patterns that pulse with dark energy. His eyes become pools of molten lava, burning with the fury of the underworld. Massive horns sprout from his forehead, curving menacingly above his head. His fingers elongate into razor-sharp claws, and his teeth grow into jagged fangs capable of ripping through flesh and bone.

Standing before Shakhti, Venan is a force to be reckoned with. But even in this form, he knows he's at a disadvantage. Shakhti's power is ancient, vast, and immeasurable. But Venan—Arjun—will not back down. He's fought his father before, and he'll do it again.

Shakhti sneers at Venan's transformation, his eyes glowing with malice. "So, you choose to fight. Very well, Venan. Let us see if you have the strength to stand against your creator!"

With a deafening roar, Shakhti swings his staff, unleashing a wave of dark energy that crashes toward Venan like a tidal wave. Venan braces himself, crossing his arms in front of him as the energy slams into him, sending him skidding backward across the cracked earth. The force of the attack is immense, but Venan grits his teeth and holds his ground, the energy dissipating around him.

Venan's lava-filled eyes lock onto Shakhti, and with a burst of speed, he charges forward, claws extended. He slashes at Shakhti with ferocious precision, each strike aimed at vital points. But Shakhti is no ordinary demon—he's the supreme demon, and he parries Venan's attacks with ease, his staff moving like a blur as it deflects every blow.

The two demons clash in a storm of violence, their battle shaking the very foundations of the Dark World. Each strike from Venan is met with an equally powerful counter from Shakhti, and soon, the air is thick with the sounds of their roars and the crackling of dark energy.

Venan summons a torrent of hellfire, sending it surging toward Shakhti. The flames scorch the earth, leaving a trail of molten rock in their wake. But Shakhti merely raises a hand, and the hellfire dissipates as if it were nothing more than smoke in the wind.

"You're weak, Venan!" Shakhti taunts, his voice booming. "You cannot defeat me. You're nothing more than a shadow of your true potential!"

Venan snarls, refusing to be cowed. He channels more of his dark energy, his body glowing with a crimson aura as he gathers his strength for another attack. But as he prepares to strike, Shakhti suddenly appears behind him, moving with impossible speed. Before Venan can react, Shakhti drives his staff into Venan's back, sending a surge of dark energy coursing through his body.

Venan cries out in pain, his knees buckling as the energy tears through him, threatening to rip him apart from the inside. He collapses to the ground, his strength fading as the darkness overwhelms him.

Shakhti looms over him, his expression one of triumph. "Do you see now, Venan? You cannot win. You belong to me. Surrender, and I may yet allow you to live as my servant."

Venan struggles to rise, his body trembling with the effort. He knows he's outmatched, but he refuses to give in. With a defiant growl, he forces himself to his feet, his eyes blazing with determination.

"I'll never surrender to you," Venan spits, his voice filled with venom. "I'll fight you until my last breath!"

Shakhti's expression darkens, his patience wearing thin. "Then you will die, Venan. And I will take what is rightfully mine."

He raises his staff, ready to deliver the final blow. But before he can strike, a powerful shockwave ripples through the air, forcing Shakhti to stumble backward. The ground beneath them quakes, and the shadows around them writhe and twist as if something immense is approaching.

Venan, barely able to stand, looks up in confusion. The air crackles with energy, and suddenly, a figure emerges from the darkness—a demon.

The newcomer is taller and more imposing than Shakhti, his presence commanding and awe-inspiring. His skin is a deep, shimmering black, like polished obsidian, and his eyes are twin orbs of blazing blue fire. His horns are longer and sharper than Venan's.

The Dark World, a place of endless shadows and unimaginable horrors, now bears witness to an unexpected turn of events. As the mysterious figure emerges from the darkness, the very air around him crackles with raw power. Shakhti, the supreme demon, falters for the first time in millennia, his eyes narrowing as he takes in the sight before him.

The demon who stands before them is massive, towering even over Shakhti himself. His horns curving wickedly above his head, and his presence radiates a terrifying aura of authority and power.

Shakhti's eyes widen in recognition, a rare expression of shock crossing his usually impassive face. "Beren..." he mutters, his voice tinged with a mixture of surprise and dread.

Venan, struggling to stay on his feet, looks up at the newcomer in disbelief. The name strikes a chord deep within him—a name he hasn't heard in years, one he thought was lost to the depths of the Dark World. Beren, his elder brother, a being of immense power and the only one who could ever rival Shakhti.

Beren steps forward, his movements smooth and deliberate. He surveys the scene before him, his blazing blue eyes settling on Venan for a brief moment before turning to Shakhti. There is no warmth in his gaze, only a cold, calculating intensity.

"Father," Beren says, his voice deep and resonant, carrying a weight that seems to press down on everything around him. "It has been a long time."

Shakhti recovers quickly, his expression hardening as he straightens up, attempting to reclaim his dominant posture. "Beren," he acknowledges, his voice laced with irritation. "I did not expect to see you here."

"And yet, here I am," Beren replies coolly. "It seems you've overstepped once again, Shakhti. You should have known that your time of unchecked dominance would not last forever."

Shakhti snarls, the ground beneath him cracking as his anger flares. "You dare challenge me, boy? I am the supreme demon! You are nothing more than a wayward child who abandoned his true purpose."

Beren's eyes flash dangerously, the blue flames within them intensifying. "I have not abandoned anything, Shakhti. I have simply been waiting—waiting for the right moment to correct the mistakes you've made."

Venan watches the exchange, his breath coming in ragged gasps as he tries to gather his strength. The power radiating from Beren is overwhelming, and he can feel the tide of battle shifting in his favor. His brother is not one to be trifled with, and even Shakhti seems to recognize the threat he now faces.

Shakhti's grip tightens on his obsidian staff, the runes along its surface glowing with dark energy. "You think you can defeat me? I created you, Beren! I am your father, your master!"

Beren's expression remains impassive. "You are my father, yes. But you are not my master. You never were."

With those words, Beren lunges forward, moving with incredible speed and precision. His obsidian claws slash through the air, leaving trails of blue fire in their wake. Shakhti barely has time to react before Beren is upon him, their battle erupting in a violent clash of power and fury.

Shakhti swings his staff with deadly force, dark energy crackling as it collides with Beren's claws. The impact sends shockwaves through the Dark World, causing the ground to tremble and the skies to roil with storm clouds. Beren's strength is immense, each blow delivered with the weight of centuries of pent-up anger and resentment.

Venan watches in awe as Beren drives Shakhti back, their father's usual composure faltering under the relentless assault. Beren's attacks are swift and calculated, each strike aimed with deadly precision. For the first time, Shakhti appears to be on the defensive, his movements growing more frantic as he tries to keep up with his son's ferocity.

"You cannot win, Shakhti!" Beren roars, his voice echoing through the darkened landscape. "Your reign of terror ends here!"

Shakhti's eyes blaze with fury, but there's a hint of something else—fear. He channels all his energy into a desperate counterattack, summoning a massive wave of dark energy that surges toward Beren like a tidal wave. But Beren meets it head-on, his obsidian claws slicing through the energy as if it were nothing more than mist.

The battle rages on, the sky above them darkening as if the very fabric of the Dark World is being torn apart by their conflict. Shakhti's attacks grow more erratic, his strength waning as Beren continues to press the advantage. Each clash of their powers sends ripples through the air, distorting reality around them.

Finally, with a powerful sweep of his arm, Beren strikes Shakhti across the chest, sending him crashing into a jagged outcropping of rock. Shakhti gasps in pain, the impact leaving deep cracks in the ground beneath him. He struggles to rise, but the weight of his defeat is evident in his eyes.

Beren looms over him, his blue fire eyes burning with an intensity that leaves no room for mercy. "This is the end, Shakhti. You have lost."

Shakhti, breathing heavily, glares up at Beren with hatred. But he knows he's beaten, and the realization is like a bitter poison in his veins. His lips curl into a snarl, but there's no defiance left in him. Only the cold, harsh truth that he cannot win this fight.

Without a word, Shakhti's form begins to waver, his body flickering as if it's being consumed by shadows. He stares at Beren for a long moment; his eyes filled with a mixture of anger and regret. Then, with a final, venomous glare, Shakhti vanishes into the darkness, his presence evaporating like smoke on the wind.

Beren watches him disappear, his expression unreadable. The battle is over, but the victory is bittersweet. He knows that Shakhti will return—his father is not one to accept defeat lightly. But for now, the threat has been neutralized.

Venan, still weak from his own battle, collapses to the ground, his demonic form flickering as he struggles to maintain it. Beren turns to him, his expression softening slightly as he approaches.

"Venan," Beren says quietly, his voice losing some of its harshness. "You fought well. But you are not yet ready to face Shakhti alone."

Venan looks up at his brother, his eyes filled with exhaustion and a grudging respect. "Thank you, Beren," he mutters, his voice hoarse. "I wouldn't have made it without you."

Beren nods, extending a hand to help Venan to his feet. "You are strong, Venan. But strength alone will not be enough. You must learn to control the darkness within you, to harness it without letting it consume you."

Venan takes his brother's hand, rising unsteadily to his feet. "I know," he replies, his voice filled with determination. "And I will. But for now, we need to regroup. Shakhti won't stay hidden for long."

Beren's eyes flicker with a knowing light. "Indeed. But when he returns, we will be ready. Together, we will put an end to his reign once and for all."

With that, the two brothers stand side by side, their gazes fixed on the dark horizon. The battle is far from over, but for the first time in a long time, there is hope. Hope that the darkness can be overcome, that the bonds of blood can be forged into something stronger—something capable of challenging even the mightiest of demons.

As the shadows of the Dark World begin to recede, Venan and Beren prepare for the battles yet to come, knowing that together, they are a force to be reckoned with.

Venan, still in his demonic form, looks at his elder brother Beren, who stands tall and resolute beside him. The flickering shadows around them seem to acknowledge the shift in power, the dominance of the two brothers evident in the uneasy calm that has settled over the hellish landscape.

Venan's mind races. Though they had driven Shakhti away, he knows his father well enough to understand that this victory is only temporary. Shakhti will return, more determined and vengeful than ever. Waiting for his inevitable return is not an option.

Venan turns to Beren, his eyes burning with purpose. "We can't stay here, Beren. If we wait for Shakhti to make his next move, we'll only be giving him time to regain his strength and plot his revenge. We need to take the fight to him—but not here, not in the Dark World."

Beren's intense blue eyes meet Venan's, a flicker of curiosity mixed with caution. "Where do you suggest we go, brother? Shakhti's reach extends far beyond this realm."

Venan nods, his expression determined. "I know. That's why we need to take him by surprise—hit him where he's least expecting it. We'll go to Earth. He has found a strong host for his soul. It belongs to the earth. We cannot fight him but we can trap him. There, we can regroup, strategize, and strike before he even knows what's coming."

Beren's brow furrows slightly as he considers Venan's plan. "Earth is not without its dangers, Venan. The gods and other forces there may not welcome us, especially if they learn of our presence. And there is the matter of maintaining control over our powers in that realm. The balance between light and darkness is more precarious there."

Venan smirks, a hint of his usual defiance returning. "I've been on Earth before, Beren. I know how to navigate its complexities. And you—well, your power is unmatched. Together, we can handle whatever challenges come our way. Besides, the humans there are embroiled in their own struggles. They won't even notice us if we're careful."

Beren's gaze shifts to the dark horizon, the remnants of their battle with Shakhti still visible in the distance. He knows Venan is right—waiting here in the Dark World is too risky. Shakhti's return is inevitable, and when he comes back, it will be with a vengeance. But on Earth, they might just have the advantage.

"Very well," Beren says, his voice resolute. " But we must be cautious."

Venan grins, his confidence bolstered by Beren's agreement. "Caution is my middle name," he jokes, though the seriousness of the situation is not lost on him. "But seriously, we'll be careful. We'll strike hard and fast, and Shakhti won't know what hit him."

With their decision made, Venan takes a step forward, raising his hand as he begins to summon the power within him. The air around them crackles with energy as he concentrates, the dark flames of his demonic aura swirling around him. He feels the familiar pull of his teleportation ability, the connection to Earth already forming in his mind.

Beren watches silently, his expression unreadable. He's always been the more stoic of the two, the one who thinks things through before acting. But in this moment, he trusts Venan's instincts, knowing that their best chance at defeating Shakhti lies in taking the fight to a place where their father's power is less absolute.

As the portal begins to form, a swirling vortex of darkness opening before them, Venan looks at Beren one last time. "Ready?"

Beren nods, his obsidian claws glowing faintly with blue fire. "Ready."

Without another word, the two brothers step into the portal, the darkness of the Dark World giving way to a rushing sensation of movement as they are transported across realms. The world around them blurs, shifting from the bleak, shadowed landscape of their home to the vibrant, chaotic energy of Earth.

When the sensation finally stops, Venan and Beren find themselves standing in a dense, shadowy forest on Earth. The night sky above them is clear, the stars shining brightly in stark contrast to the oppressive darkness they left behind. The air is fresh, filled with the sounds of rustling leaves and distant wildlife.

Venan takes a deep breath, his senses adjusting to the new environment. It's been a while since he was last on Earth, but the familiarity of it is comforting. He looks around, ensuring that they've arrived unnoticed, and then turns to Beren.

"This is it," Venan says quietly. "From here, we plan our next move. Shakhti will eventually find out we're here, but by then, we'll be ready to face him—and to end this once and for all."

Beren nods, his eyes scanning the surroundings. "We'll need to stay hidden, gather information, and strike with precision. Shakhti will expect brute force, but we'll give him something far more calculated."

Venan's grin returns, a dangerous glint in his eyes. "Exactly. Let's get to work."

Together, the brothers begin to move through the forest, their forms shifting slightly to blend into the shadows. They are demons, powerful beyond measure, but here on Earth, they must be as much strategists as warriors. The battle against Shakhti is far from over, but now, with the element of surprise on their side, they are one step closer to ending his reign.

As they disappear into the night, the forest remains still, unaware of the two powerful beings who have just arrived. The stars continue to shine above, indifferent to the cosmic battle that is about to unfold on this unsuspecting planet.

But for Venan and Beren, the stars are merely a backdrop to the real conflict—the one that will determine the fate of not just their world, but perhaps the entire universe.

It's late evening in Mumbai, the city buzzing with life as always. But inside a dimly lit warehouse on the outskirts, the atmosphere is tense, filled with anticipation. Amar and Jay stand near a table cluttered with maps and documents, their expressions grim as they discuss the latest intelligence on Javed Ustad's plans being outsmarted.

Suddenly, a ripple of energy fills the air, causing both men to look up in alarm. A dark portal begins to form in the center of the room, swirling with a mixture of shadows and flickering flames. Jay instinctively reaches for his weapon, while Amar tenses, ready for whatever might emerge.

From the portal, two figures step out. The first is familiar—Venan, though they know him as Arjun, his expression as intense as ever. But the second figure is a stranger. Beren obtained a host as they both entered the earth.

Jay's grip on his weapon tightens, and Amar's eyes widen in shock. But before they can react, Venan raises a hand, signaling them to stand down.

"It's okay," Venan says, his voice calm but commanding. "He's with me."

Amar, still wary, looks between the two demons. "Arjun... who is this?"

"This," Venan replies, turning to the towering figure beside him, "is Beren, my elder brother. He's here to help us."

Beren nods in acknowledgment, his gaze sweeping over Amar and Jay with a penetrating intensity. There's a moment of silence, the tension in the room thick enough to cut with a knife.

Jay finally lowers his weapon, though he remains on edge. "Brother? You didn't mention you had a brother."

Venan offers a small, almost apologetic smile. "There's a lot I haven't mentioned. But right now, what's important is that Beren is on our side. With his help, we have a much better chance of stopping Shakhti."

Amar steps forward, his eyes still studying Beren with cautious curiosity. "If he's anything like you, Arjun, then I suppose we should be grateful."

Beren's expression softens slightly, a flicker of something akin to respect passing through his fiery gaze. "You have my word," he says, his deep voice resonating through the room, "I am here to fight alongside you. Shakhti is a threat to us all, and I will do whatever it takes to ensure his defeat."

Amar nods, though there's still a hint of unease in his demeanor. "We'll need all the help we can get. If you're with us, then welcome."

Jay, though still cautious, gives a nod as well. "Just don't expect us to keep up with whatever it is you two can do."

Venan chuckles, the tension in the room easing slightly. "Don't worry, Jay. We'll handle the heavy lifting. You just focus on what you do best."

With that, the initial introductions are complete. Though the situation is far from normal, there's a growing sense of unity in the room. Venan and Beren, two powerful demons, have now joined forces with Amar and Jay, forming a formidable alliance against the looming threat of Shakhti and Javed.

• • •

"Amar's mind churned with questions, but one thing was clear: something, or someone, was out there with abilities that rivaled even Arjun's. And they had just played a crucial, yet mysterious, role in saving countless lives. But the mystery deepened the more Amar thought about it. If this figure wasn't Arjun, then what were they after, and why did they intervene now?"

CHAPTER **NINE** THE GREAT ALLIANCE

It was three days before Indian Independence Day. The humid air outside Arthur Brown's research facility was thick with the tension he had been feeling for days. The unease gnawed at him, a constant reminder that something was amiss. Shakhti's presence had been like a shadow in the corner of his mind, faint yet unmistakable. Arthur, or rather Amon, had lived many lives, but this mission felt different. The need to find Shakhti was an itch he couldn't scratch, and India seemed to be where the answers lay.

Arthur was packing his bags in his modest apartment, carefully placing files and equipment into his suitcase. He paused, staring out of the window. The sun was setting, casting a fiery glow over the skyline. He picked up his phone and dialed Eric's number.

"Eric, it's time. Pack your bags; we're off to India," Arthur said, his voice steady but laced with urgency.

"India? What's this about, Arthur? I thought we were still working on the—"

"Change of plans. There's something I need to investigate. We'll call it a technical meeting for the research facility, but the real reason… it's more complicated. Just be ready."

Eric hesitated for a moment before responding, "Alright, give us half an hour."

Arthur ended the call, his mind racing. This trip was more than just a break from his research facility. It was an opportunity to explore India, to search for Shakhti under the guise of a professional visit. Amon's godly aura kept him hidden from Shakhti's detection, but it also made Shakhti's presence detectable to him. What Amon didn't realize, however, was that Shakhti's sons—Arjun and Beren—were also nearby, their energies blending with their father's, causing confusion in Amon's perception.

As the evening darkened, Arthur slung his bag over his shoulder and took a deep breath. The cab was waiting downstairs. He locked his apartment door and headed out, the cool evening air brushing against his face as he walked to the vehicle.

The driver nodded as Arthur approached. "To Eric's apartment," Arthur instructed.

The cab ride was silent except for the hum of the engine. The city lights flickered past, a blur of motion as Arthur's thoughts wandered to the days ahead. Shakhti was out there, somewhere, and Amon was determined to find him.

The cab arrived at Eric's apartment building. Eric was already waiting at the entrance, a suitcase by his side. He looked up as the cab pulled in, a mixture of concern and curiosity on his face.

"Arthur," Eric greeted as he loaded his bag into the boot, "You've got me worried. What's really going on?"

"I'll explain everything on the plane. For now, let's just get to the airport."

Eric nodded, his unease palpable, but he trusted Arthur enough to follow his lead without further questions. The cab sped off into the night, heading toward the international airport.

The flight was long but uneventful. The soft hum of the airplane engines and the dimmed cabin lights had allowed Arthur to think, to plan. Eric had dozed off somewhere over the Indian Ocean, but Arthur couldn't sleep. His mind was too occupied with the task ahead.

The plane touched down at Chhatrapati Shivaji Maharaj International Airport just before dawn. The city of Mumbai was beginning to stir, the first rays of sunlight creeping over the horizon. As Arthur and Eric disembarked, the humid air of the city hit them, a sharp contrast to the climate-controlled cabin they had just left.

Arthur adjusted the strap of his bag as they made their way through the bustling terminal. It was then that he noticed something unusual. Soldiers, heavily armed, were patrolling the area. Their presence was conspicuous, a sign that something was not quite right.

"Eric, do you see that?" Arthur whispered, nodding towards a group of soldiers who were speaking into their radios with urgent expressions.

"Yeah, I noticed. Looks like they're preparing for something. Maybe a drill?" Eric replied, though his tone suggested he wasn't convinced.

Arthur's eyes narrowed. This wasn't normal. Even on the brink of Independence Day celebrations, this level of military activity was excessive. His instincts told him that Shakhti—or something related to him—was involved.

They approached the immigration counters, but Arthur's focus was elsewhere. He was scanning the crowd, looking for anything out of place, anything that might give him a clue.

"Let's keep a low profile," Arthur suggested. "We'll figure out what's going on after we get settled."

As they cleared immigration and stepped into the arrivals hall, Arthur felt a subtle shift in the atmosphere. The air seemed thicker, charged with an energy he couldn't quite place. It was faint, but it was there—Shakhti's presence, or at least what he thought was Shakhti's presence, was nearby.

A sense of urgency gripped him. The search for Shakhti was no longer just a mission; it was a race against time. Little did Amon know, he was not just sensing Shakhti, but also his sons, who were closer than he could have imagined.

"Eric, stay close. Things might get complicated from here on out," Arthur warned as they made their way towards the exit.

The city of Mumbai awaited them, a sprawling, chaotic metropolis where anything could happen. And Arthur knew that somewhere within its vast expanse, his destiny—and that of the world—was about to be decided.

#

The tension was palpable as the chaos unfolded at Chhatrapati Shivaji International Airport. Amar and Jay, both drenched in sweat, had just received a harrowing message: a small but potent bomb had been planted somewhere in the sprawling airport, set to detonate within minutes. The clock was ticking, and the airport buzzed with the frantic efforts of the military and bomb squads.

As military officers combed the terminal, one of them noticed something suspicious—a dustbin, tucked away in a less-trafficked corner. It looked ordinary, but in situations like these, nothing was taken for granted. The officer's heart pounded as he radioed in, his voice steady but laced with urgency, "I think I've found it. Dustbin near Gate 27. Could be the bomb."

Amar, nearby, heard the call and sprinted towards the bin, summoning the bomb squad to confirm the officer's suspicion. Within seconds, the area was swarming with heavily armed military personnel, their presence a stark contrast to the confused and frightened civilians being swiftly evacuated. Arthur and Eric, who had been observing the situation unfold from a distance, felt the gravity of the situation deepen. But before they could fully grasp what was happening, an officer urgently pushed them back towards safety.

The bomb squad approached the dustbin cautiously, instruments and sensors in hand. After several tense minutes, their worst fears were confirmed—it was a bomb, and a complex one at that. The squad leader, beads of sweat forming on his brow, took a step back and exchanged worried glances with his team. "We can't defuse this," he whispered, the words barely escaping his lips.

Panic rippled through the ranks. With just over a minute left on the timer, they had to act fast. The only option was to move the bomb to the runway, an open area where the explosion would cause the least damage. But there was no guarantee they'd make it in time.

A brave officer, steely-eyed and resolute, stepped forward. "Sir, I'll take it from here," he said, his voice firm and unwavering.

"Are you sure, officer?" the Major asked, his tone grave, knowing the risk was almost certain death.

"One hundred percent, Sir!" the officer replied, his confidence undeniable.

Without hesitation, the officer lifted the dustbin and placed it inside a nearby taxiing cart. He jumped into the driver's seat; his knuckles white as he gripped the wheel. The cart moved, but it was slow, far too slow. The seconds ticked away mercilessly.

As the timer hit ten seconds, the officer realized he was still too close to several parked planes. Desperation surged through him, and he slammed his foot on the accelerator, pushing the cart to its limits. The engine whined, but the cart gained speed.

Then, with just two seconds left, something extraordinary happened.

A man, glowing with an ethereal bluish light, appeared out of nowhere, his figure a blur of motion. He moved with lightning speed, snatching the bin from the cart just as the timer neared its final moment. With a swift, powerful motion, he hurled the bomb into the open area of the runway.

Before the officer could even process what was happening, the mysterious figure waved his hand towards the sky. From above, a swirling mass of water materialized, descending like a vortex. It was a water tornado, twisting and roaring as it enveloped the explosion. The blast was muffled; the flames smothered instantly by the cascading water. The fiery threat was neutralized before it could cause any harm.

In the aftermath, as the water settled and the danger passed, the glowing figure vanished as suddenly as he had appeared. The officer, still gripping the cart's steering wheel, stared in disbelief at the now calm runway. He couldn't comprehend what he had just witnessed.

"What just happened?" he muttered, his heart still racing. But there was no answer, only the faint echo of the water's final droplets hitting the tarmac. The airport was safe, but the mystery of the blue-glowing man lingered in the air, an enigma that would haunt the officer's thoughts long after the adrenaline faded.

As the chaos at Chhatrapati Shivaji International Airport subsided, Amar stood among the scattered debris, his mind racing. The image of the glowing figure who had saved them all played over and over in his head. There was something familiar about the way the figure moved, the effortless power, the confidence. It struck him suddenly—could it have been Arjun?

But the thought didn't make sense. Arjun, or rather Venan, along with his brother Beren, was supposed to be on the other side of the city, dealing with a far more pressing threat. The two brothers were tracking down the last packet of RDX, the only one still unaccounted for, hidden somewhere in the densely populated heart of Mumbai. The other two had already been secured by the police, but this final bomb posed the greatest danger. How could Arjun have been here?

Amar's thoughts were interrupted by the buzz of his phone. It was Arjun.

"Arjun, was that you at the airport?" Amar asked without preamble, his voice edged with urgency.

There was a brief pause on the other end before Arjun replied, his tone steady. "No, Amar. I'm with Beren, handling the situation in Mumbai. We've just secured the last packet of RDX."

"Then who...?" Amar's voice trailed off, the pieces not fitting together. If it wasn't Arjun, then who had saved them?

"I don't know," Arjun replied, his voice carrying a note of concern. "But whoever it was, they have power—serious power. I think whom we are searching for is in a search of us."

Amar's mind churned with questions, but one thing was clear: something, or someone, was out there with abilities that rivaled even Arjun's. And they had just played a crucial, yet mysterious, role in saving countless lives. But the mystery deepened the more Amar thought about it. If this figure wasn't Arjun, then what were they after, and why did they intervene now?

"Be careful, Amar," Arjun added before the call ended. "We're dealing with more than just bombs now."

As the line went dead, Amar looked around the still-smoking runway, the scene eerily calms after the earlier chaos. The threat of the bomb might be over, but a new, unknown player had entered the game.

#

As the adrenaline of the airport incident began to fade, Arthur and Eric found themselves in the back of a classic Indian taxi, the vibrant streets of Mumbai unfolding around them. The city was a whirlwind of sights, sounds, and smells, a stark contrast to the tense atmosphere they had just left behind. Despite the intensity of the situation, Arthur couldn't help but feel a sense of excitement as they made their way to meet an old friend—Dr. Arman, a nuclear scientist working at BARC (Bhabha Atomic Research Centre).

The taxi wove through the bustling traffic, honking at every turn, before finally pulling up outside a modest yet well-kept home in a quiet neighborhood. Arthur and Eric stepped out, thanking the driver in their distinctly British accents, which garnered a smile from the curious locals.

The door to the house opened before they could knock, and Dr. Arman, a tall, bespectacled man with a warm smile, greeted them. His eyes lit up as he saw Arthur. "Arthur! It's been too long, my friend," he exclaimed, pulling him into a hug. He then turned to Eric, shaking his hand warmly. "Welcome, Eric. It's a pleasure to finally meet you."

"Good to see you, Arman," Arthur replied, his voice relaxed after the long journey. "It's been too long indeed."

"Come in, come in," Arman insisted, leading them into his home. The smell of freshly brewed chai wafted through the air, and the house was a cozy blend of modern comforts and traditional Indian decor. "I've prepared a little something to welcome you both," Arman added with a grin.

After a few moments of exchanging pleasantries and enjoying the hospitality, Arthur excused himself to freshen up after the long flight. When he returned, he carried a neatly bound set of papers in his hand.

"Arman, I brought something for you," Arthur said, handing over the documents.

Arman accepted the papers with a curious glance. "What's this?"

"These are the details of two new radioactive elements we've discovered," Arthur explained. "They were collected from meteor samples in the Valley of the Kings, Egypt. They're more powerful than anything we're currently using for power generation."

Arman's eyes widened as he skimmed through the papers, his interest clearly piqued. "This is incredible," he murmured, his mind already racing with possibilities. "If these materials are as potent as you say, they could revolutionize our approach to nuclear energy."

He looked up at Arthur, his expression serious. "We need to discuss this in detail, but it's best we do so in the lab where we have the proper equipment to analyze these findings."

Arthur nodded in agreement. "That's what I was hoping you'd say."

Arman smiled, his earlier warmth returning. “But before we dive into this, I want you both to take a day off. You’ve had a long journey, and it’s not every day you get to experience Mumbai. Go out, see the city, and relax. We’ll get started first thing tomorrow.”

Eric, who had been quietly observing, chimed in with a grin. “I wouldn’t mind a bit of exploring.”

Arthur smiled, appreciating the hospitality. “Thanks, Arman. We’ll take you up on that offer.”

“Excellent!” Arman said, his eyes twinkling. “Mumbai has a lot to offer, and you’ll need your energy for what’s to come. But don’t worry, we’ll get to the science soon enough.”

With that, the three friends enjoyed the rest of the evening, catching up and enjoying the warm hospitality. But even as they laughed and shared stories, Arthur’s mind kept drifting back to the papers, eager to uncover the potential locked within those new elements.

#

The night was quiet at Dr. Arman's house, the atmosphere warm with the lingering scents of Indian spices and the hum of distant city life. Arthur, Eric, and Arman sat at the dining table, enjoying a late meal and discussing old memories. The conversation flowed easily, the earlier tension of the day melting away with each shared laugh.

But the peace was short-lived.

Arjun and Beren had been tracking their target all day. They had watched the CCTV footage repeatedly, the image of Arthur slipping through a crowd and dissolving into a blue hue burned into their minds. Arjun's instincts told him that this man wasn't ordinary, and he needed to know who, or what, he was.

The two brothers moved swiftly and silently through the shadows; their demonic auras cloaked to avoid detection. They reached the house, the faint glow of lights seeping through the curtains. With a nod to each other, they prepared to break in.

Inside, Arthur paused mid-sentence, his fork hovering just above his plate. His senses, honed over millennia, picked up on something—no, someone. Two powerful auras, dark and dangerous, approaching rapidly. His eyes narrowed, the god within him stirring, ready to defend.

Without warning, the front door exploded inward, wood splintering and metal hinges snapping as Arjun and Beren burst into the room. The force of their entry sent shockwaves through the house, knocking over furniture and shattering glass.

Arthur was already on his feet, the blue hue of his divine power flickering to life around him. He didn't need to ask who they were; their presence was unmistakable—demons. And not just any demons, but ones with a formidable power that rivaled his own.

"You should've stayed out of this," Arjun growled, his eyes glowing with a fierce intensity as he and Beren charged forward.

But Arthur, or rather Amon, was quicker. In an instant, he lunged at the two brothers, grabbing them by their throats and slamming them through the remains of the door. The force of the impact sent all three crashing into the yard, the ground cracking beneath them.

The battle was fierce and fast. Amon's power radiated in blue waves, each strike from his fists sending shockwaves through the air. Arjun countered with bursts of fire, his own aura flaring with a fiery red glow, while Beren's strength was monstrous, his blows leaving deep craters in the earth.

For a while, it seemed they were evenly matched. Amon's divine speed and precision clashed with the raw power and fury of the demon brothers. But as the fight raged on, Amon began to sense something—an absence, a void where a familiar, despised aura should have been.

He paused, dodging another fiery attack from Arjun, and studied them more closely. These were demons, yes, but not the one he had been hunting for so long. Not Shakhti.

Realization dawned on him as he caught Beren's wrist mid-swing, holding it effortlessly in the air. "You're not with him," Amon said, his voice calm but tinged with the surprise of this revelation.

Arjun, breathing heavily from the exertion, met Amon's gaze. "We have no love for Shakhti. We want him dead just as much as you do."

Amon released his grip, stepping back, his aura fading slightly as he processed this new information. The tension in the air thickened with confusion and uncertainty.

"You're hunting him too?" Amon asked, his voice quieter now, more controlled.

"Yes," Beren replied, rubbing his wrist where Amon's grip had been. "He is our father. And he needs to be stopped."

For a moment, the three powerful beings stood in silence, the night air thick with the remnants of their battle. Amon's divine form still glowed faintly, but the hostility had drained from his stance. He had spent so long fighting enemies that the thought of allies—especially demonic ones—was foreign to him.

Finally, Amon nodded. "If that's the case, we're on the same side. But if you ever come after me again, I won't hesitate to end it."

Arjun smirked, wiping blood from the corner of his mouth. "Fair enough. But next time, don't make it so easy to track you down." His wound heals.

With that, the tension eased. The three of them, each powerful in their own right, stood down. What had started as a confrontation between enemies had unexpectedly turned into an uneasy alliance against a common foe—Shakhti.

•••

"The transition was jarring, as if they were being pulled through the very fabric of existence. When the chaos subsided, they found themselves standing on a barren landscape under a sky that churned with ominous clouds and streaks of crimson lightning. The ground beneath them was cracked and charred, exuding a sense of malevolence that seeped into the air."

CHAPTER

TEN THE BETRAYAL

After fixing the door to Dr. Arman's home with a swift gesture, Arthur, now fully revealing his identity as Amon, nodded to Arjun and Beren. The tension between them had dissipated, replaced by a fragile alliance against the greater threat of Shakhti. Together, they moved with purpose, teleporting to the police station where Amar and Jay awaited.

The station was buzzing with activity, a mixture of police officers, detectives, and civilians moving through the space. Amar was seated at his desk, surrounded by stacks of reports and photos from various crime scenes. Jay, sitting nearby, was immersed in a file, his brow furrowed in concentration.

When the door to the station creaked open, both Amar and Jay looked up. Their eyes widened in surprise as they saw Amon, flanked by Arjun and Beren. The presence of the godlike figure seemed to command the attention of everyone in the room.

Amar quickly stood, his expression a mix of awe and relief. "Amon," he said, his voice carrying the weight of their collective hopes. "I never thought I'd see you here, standing with us. You're the hope we've been waiting for."

Jay, however, set the file he was holding aside and stepped forward, his demeanor more focused and urgent. "This is a game-changer, no doubt," he acknowledged, glancing between Amon, Arjun, and Beren. "But we need to prioritize. Shakhti is still out there, and he's the real threat. We can't afford to get distracted by anything else—not even the mystery of those dead bodies. We need to stop him before he can do any more damage."

Amar nodded in agreement, his gaze turning serious. "Jay's right. Shakhti's our main target now. Everything else can wait."

Amon, sensing the gravity of the situation, gave a solemn nod. "You're right. Shakhti's plans must be stopped at all costs. But we must stay vigilant—those other mysteries could be connected, and we can't leave any stone unturned."

Arthur, fully embodying his divine persona as Amon, stepped forward, his presence commanding the room. Amar and Jay, still processing the magnitude of what had just unfolded, watched as Arthur's eyes gleamed with a quiet intensity.

"Amar, Jay," Arthur began, his voice calm but laced with authority. "Shakhti is not just a criminal—he's a force of darkness that goes beyond anything humanity has faced. But this is not your battle to fight. You've done more than anyone could have asked, and now it's time for you to step back."

Amar opened his mouth to protest, but Arthur raised a hand to silence him gently. "I know what you're thinking. You've faced dangers, uncovered secrets, and saved countless lives. But Shakhti... he's not just another enemy. His power is ancient, and his reach is far beyond this world. Arjun, Beren, and I—we are uniquely equipped to handle him."

Arjun, standing tall with his arms crossed, nodded in agreement. "We've been dealing with threats like him for eons. This isn't just a battle; it's a war that's been waged for centuries."

Beren, his eyes glowing with a fierce, otherworldly light, added, "We won't let him win. Not this time. But we need to focus all our efforts on him. If you're tangled up in this, it'll only slow us down and put you at risk."

Jay, sensing the inevitability of what was being asked of them, exhaled deeply. "So, what do you want us to do?"

Arthur's expression softened, though his resolve remained firm. "Focus on maintaining order here. Keep the city safe, manage the aftermath of Javed's plans, and ensure that no one else gets hurt. We'll take care of Shakhti. This isn't your burden to bear."

Amar, though reluctant, knew that Arthur was right. He nodded slowly, the weight of responsibility shifting off his shoulders, replaced by a trust in Amon's ability to protect them all.

"We'll do as you ask," Amar said, his voice steady. "But if you need anything—anything at all—you call us. We won't hesitate to support you in any way we can."

Arthur smiled, a rare warmth touching his features. "I know I can count on you. But for now, trust us to finish this. When it's over, the world will be safer—and that's a promise."

With that, Arthur turned to Arjun and Beren, his expression hardening once more. "Let's end this."

As they prepared to leave, Amar and Jay watched them, a mix of hope and worry in their eyes. The three figures—Amon, Arjun, and Beren—disappeared in a flash of light, leaving behind a room that now felt strangely empty, yet filled with the promise of an impending victory.

#

Beren's eyes flickered with an intense blue flame as he extended his hand toward Arthur and Arjun. The space around them began to warp, reality itself bending to Beren's will. Within seconds, the trio was engulfed in a swirling vortex of shadows and flames, leaving the world they knew far behind. They were traveling to the Dark World—a realm of ancient power, where the boundaries between life and death, time and space, were blurred.

The transition was jarring, as if they were being pulled through the very fabric of existence. When the chaos subsided, they found themselves standing on a barren landscape under a sky that churned with ominous clouds and streaks of crimson lightning. The ground beneath them was cracked and charred, exuding a sense of malevolence that seeped into the air.

"This is where we last faced Shakhti," Beren said, his voice echoing with a blend of anger and sorrow. "The battle here was brutal, but we managed to drive him away. I hoped that would be the end of him... but it seems he's found a way to survive."

Arjun, in his true form as Venan, clenched his fists, his aura radiating with barely contained fury. "He's more cunning than we thought. We should have destroyed him when we had the chance."

Arthur, standing between them as Amon, closed his eyes, drawing on the vast reservoir of his divine power. The energy coursed through him, connecting him to the fabric of the universe. He reached out, his mind expanding across the cosmos, searching for any trace of

Shakhti's presence. For a moment, the only sound was the crackling of the dark energy that filled the realm.

But as Amon probed deeper into the universe, his expression darkened. "I can't find him," he muttered, frustration evident in his voice. "His energy... it's completely masked. It's as if he's disappeared from existence itself."

Beren stepped forward, his eyes narrowing. "Shakhti is not one to simply vanish. If he's gone to ground, it's because he's up to something far worse. We need to think about where he would go, what he would seek."

Amon's gaze shifted to the horizon, where the landscape seemed to ripple with the remnants of the battle that had taken place here. "He's gathering power," Amon realized, his voice growing more certain. "After we drove him away, he wouldn't have gone into hiding without a purpose. He's looking for something—or someone."

Venan's fiery eyes flared as he considered Amon's words. "He was always obsessed with power. If he's left this realm, it's because he's hunting for more strength. He needs souls—life force—to sustain himself after the beating we gave him."

Amon's expression grew grim as he concentrated once more, this time not on finding Shakhti directly, but on sensing disturbances throughout the universe. He attuned his senses to the flow of energy, the rise and fall of life across countless worlds. It didn't take long before he sensed it—waves of destruction rippling through the cosmos, entire planets extinguished in a heartbeat.

"I sense... cosmic destruction," Amon said, his voice low but resonating with power. "Worlds are being torn apart.

Shakhti is consuming them, devouring the souls of entire civilizations to fuel his strength. He's preparing for something big—something that will bring him back to Earth."

Venan growled, his voice filled with rage. "He's already destroyed too much. We can't let him continue. If he's targeting Earth next, we need to be ready."

Beren nodded, his eyes blazing with determination. "Then we must stop him before he reaches our world. We need to find the source of this destruction and cut off his power before it's too late."

Amon's eyes glowed with an ethereal light as he drew in his energy, preparing to trace the destructive path Shakhti had carved across the universe. "We'll follow the trail of devastation. It will lead us to him. And when we find him, we'll end this once and for all."

With their resolve strengthened, the three figures—Amon, Venan, and Beren—prepared to embark on a journey through the darkest reaches of the universe.

They knew that Shakhti was out there, growing stronger with every soul he consumed. But they also knew that they were the only ones capable of stopping him, and they would not rest until he was defeated.

#

In the depths of a barren, otherworldly wasteland, where the sky crackled with chaotic energy and the ground pulsed with dark magic, Shakhti, now in his monstrous form as Jagtapji, stood towering over the desolate landscape. His form was an amalgamation of the countless souls and powers he had consumed—his skin was like cracked stone, glowing with the inner fire of stolen life forces, and his eyes burned with an unholy light. The air around him hummed with raw power, and even the shadows seemed to recoil from his presence.

A portal opened nearby, and from it emerged Amon, flanked by Venan and Beren. The air crackled with tension as the three figures faced Shakhti, who turned to gaze upon them with eyes full of malevolent fury.

"It's been years since I last saw you," Shakhti snarled, his voice a deep, resonant growl that seemed to shake the very ground beneath them. His gaze shifted to his sons, Venan and Beren, standing beside Amon. "Oh, my children... you could have held a special place in my empire, but instead, you've chosen to side with the gods. Have you forgotten how our families were slaughtered, their powers stolen by these gods, and yet you serve them willingly?"

Amon stepped forward, his presence radiating a calm yet formidable power. "Stop trying to twist their minds with your hatred, Shakhti," he said, his voice steady but filled with authority. "No demon was ever attacked first. You know the true story. I warned you to abandon your dark ambitions and maintain the peace. But you've already shattered that peace, and now you must face the consequences. The Almighty God will not tolerate your defiance."

Shakhti's laughter echoed through the wasteland, a harsh, grating sound that sent chills down their spines. "Who? The one who betrayed my Supreme? I no longer fear him, Amon. Today, I will end you once and for all."

Amon met his gaze, unflinching. "You've tried before, Shakhti, and you failed. Today will be no different."

Beren, his eyes blazing with an inner fire, stepped forward beside Amon. "Trust me, Father," he said, his voice cold and resolute, "this time, it won't be easy. We've grown stronger, and we won't fall to your darkness."

Shakhti's fury intensified, his aura expanding as he prepared to unleash his full might. "Then come, my children, and see if you have the strength to defy your own blood."

The ground beneath them cracked and splintered as the dark energy surrounding Shakhti surged, sending waves of power rippling through the air. Venan and Beren stood ready, their own powers flaring to life as they prepared to confront the father they had once feared but now stood against. Amon, calm and composed, began to draw on his divine energy, the light within him shining brighter as the confrontation approached.

This was it—the final confrontation between Shakhti, the fallen demon, and those who stood against his reign of terror. The fate of countless worlds, and perhaps the entire universe, hung in the balance as the battle between father and sons, between ancient darkness and divine light, was about to begin.

The air in the barren wasteland crackled with dark energy as Shakhti, now a towering figure of malevolent power, faced off against Amon, Venan, and Beren. The ground trembled beneath their feet, reflecting the immense tension in the atmosphere. This was a battle that had been brewing for centuries, and now, it was finally upon them.

With a roar that echoed across the wasteland, Shakhti launched himself at Amon, his colossal form moving with terrifying speed. The ground shattered beneath his feet as he charged, his fists glowing with the stolen power of countless souls. Amon raised his hands, summoning a shield of divine energy that shimmered with a golden light. Shakhti's fist collided with the shield, sending shockwaves rippling through the air. The force of the impact cracked the ground beneath Amon, but he held firm, his eyes locked on Shakhti's.

"You've become stronger," Amon said, his voice calm even as he struggled against the sheer force of Shakhti's attack. "But strength alone won't save you."

Shakhti snarled, pushing harder against the shield, causing it to flicker under the strain. "I've taken the power of entire worlds, Amon! I am beyond your understanding. This time, you will fall."

With a mighty push, Shakhti shattered the shield, sending Amon stumbling backward. Venan and Beren immediately moved to flank their father, their powers igniting in a brilliant display of fire and shadow. Venan unleashed a torrent of flames, his fiery aura transforming into a blazing tornado that roared toward Shakhti. At the same time, Beren summoned dark tendrils of energy, which lashed out like whips, aiming to ensnare their father.

Shakhti bellowed in rage, raising his arms to meet their assault. With a sweep of his hand, he deflected Venan's flames, turning them into a swirling vortex of dark fire that he hurled back at his son. Venan barely had time to react, conjuring a barrier of flames around himself as the dark fire collided with his shield. The impact sent him skidding across the ground, his barrier flickering but holding.

Beren's tendrils wrapped around Shakhti's limbs, tightening with an iron grip. For a moment, it seemed as though they might hold him in place. But Shakhti's power surged, and with a roar, he shattered the tendrils, the dark energy dispersing like smoke. Beren gritted his teeth, channeling more power into his attack, but Shakhti was relentless. He broke free of the tendrils, lunging at Beren with a fist charged with destructive energy.

Amon, seeing his opportunity, struck. He summoned a beam of pure divine energy, a searing column of light that descended from the heavens, aimed directly at Shakhti. The beam struck Shakhti's back with the force of a thousand suns, driving him to his knees. Shakhti howled in pain, his flesh burning under the intense light. But even as he struggled, he began to absorb the energy, his body feeding on the power.

"You can't stop me, Amon!" Shakhti roared, his voice a guttural growl as he pushed himself to his feet, the beam of light still pouring down on him. "Your power is nothing compared to mine!"

Amon poured more energy into the beam, his expression focused, but the strain was evident. "This ends now, Shakhti! Surrender, or face the wrath of the gods!"

But Shakhti was far from surrendering. With a surge of power, he broke free of the beam, sending a shockwave of dark energy that rippled through the landscape. The ground buckled and cracked, and Amon was forced to withdraw, stumbling as the shockwave hit him.

Shakhti's form shimmered with dark power as he advanced on Amon, his eyes burning with hatred. "You dare challenge me? I am the Supreme! I will tear you apart, piece by piece!"

Venan, recovering from the earlier assault, joined Beren in a renewed attack. The two brothers moved in unison; their combined power aimed at their father.

Venan unleashed another wave of fiery energy, while Beren summoned a storm of dark lightning, the bolts crackling with malevolent energy.

Shakhti laughed, a deep, menacing sound that reverberated through the air. With a gesture, he absorbed the lightning, his form glowing with the stolen energy. He deflected Venan's fire with ease, redirecting it toward Amon, who barely managed to shield himself in time.

As the battle raged, the wasteland itself seemed to be falling apart under the immense strain of their powers. The sky darkened, clouds swirling in a vortex of chaos. The ground cracked and splintered, as if unable to bear the weight of the conflict. Shakhti stood at the center of it all, his power growing with each passing moment, while Amon, Venan, and Beren struggled to keep up.

But then, something shifted in the air—a subtle change, almost imperceptible. Amon, focused on the fight, didn't notice it at first. But Shakhti did. A slow smile spread across his face as he watched Beren's movements, the way his attacks seemed to lack their usual ferocity.

"You're hesitating, Beren," Shakhti said, his voice low and taunting. "Have you forgotten where your true loyalties lie?"

Beren's eyes flickered with uncertainty, but he said nothing, continuing his assault on his father. But his strikes were slower, less focused, and Shakhti could see it. With a roar, Shakhti unleashed a blast of energy that knocked both Amon and Venan off balance, sending them crashing to the ground.

Shakhti turned his gaze to Beren, his eyes gleaming with triumph. “You know it, don’t you? The power we once had... the empire we could have built together. You were meant to rule by my side, not grovel before these so-called gods.”

Beren hesitated, his form flickering with uncertainty. Venan, struggling to his feet, noticed his brother’s hesitation. “Beren, don’t listen to him! He’s trying to manipulate you—just like he always has!”

But Beren’s expression remained conflicted, torn between his loyalty to his brother and the dark temptation his father offered. Shakhti, sensing his advantage, pressed on. “You know the truth, Beren. The gods destroyed our kind, left us to suffer while they basked in their glory. Join me, and we can take back what was stolen from us.”

Amon, realizing what was happening, struggled to stand, his energy drained from the constant assault. “Beren, you don’t have to do this. You can break free from his influence. We can end this, together.”

But Beren’s eyes had already turned to his father, a flicker of something dark and familiar passing through them. The conflict within him was evident, but the pull of his father’s words was strong. With a slow, deliberate movement, Beren stepped away from Amon and Venan, his gaze locked on Shakhti.

"Beren, no!" Venan shouted, desperation in his voice.

But it was too late. Beren had made his choice. He turned to Amon; his eyes cold, devoid of the warmth that had once been there. "I'm sorry," he said, though his tone was anything but apologetic. "But he's right. The gods took everything from us. It's time we take it back."

With a swift motion, Beren lashed out, sending a bolt of dark energy crashing into Amon. Amon, caught off guard by the betrayal, staggered backward, his defenses momentarily faltering. Shakhti laughed, a deep, triumphant sound that echoed across the battlefield.

"Welcome back, my son," Shakhti said, his voice filled with satisfaction.

Venan, his heart breaking at the sight of his brother's betrayal, felt a surge of anger and despair. But before he could act, Shakhti turned his attention to him. "And you, Venan. You've always been the weaker one. But there's still time for you to make the right choice."

Venan shook his head, his fiery aura flaring as he prepared to attack. "I'll never join you. You're a monster, and I'll see you destroyed, no matter the cost."

Shakhti sighed, as if disappointed. "So be it."

With a sudden, violent movement, Shakhti extended his hand toward Venan, a vortex of dark energy swirling in his palm. The power within it was overwhelming, a force that seemed to pull at the very fabric of existence. Venan braced himself, ready to fight to the end, but before he could react, Beren intervened, stepping in front of Shakhti.

"Father, wait," Beren said, his voice calm. "There's a better way."

Shakhti raised an eyebrow, curious. "Oh?"

Beren turned to Venan, his expression unreadable. "Venan, you know he's right. We can't win this. But we can survive. If you surrender your powers to him, he'll let us live. We can still make a difference—just not in the way you hoped."

Venan stared at his brother, a mix of betrayal and disbelief in his eyes. "You want me to give up my power? To him?"

Beren nodded, his gaze steady. "It's the only way."

Amon, still struggling to recover from Beren's attack, managed.

Venan stood frozen, his heart pounding in his chest as Beren's words sank in. The brother who had stood by his side through countless battles was now asking him to surrender his power to their father—the same father who had brought ruin to countless worlds, who had betrayed and corrupted everything they had ever stood for.

Amon, weakened but not yet defeated, pushed himself to his feet. Blood trickled from the corner of his mouth, and his once-brilliant aura was dim, flickering like a dying flame. He looked at Beren, his expression one of sorrow and disappointment. "Beren," Amon said, his voice strained, "you don't have to do this. There's still a chance to end this madness. We can stop him together."

But Beren's resolve had hardened, his eyes cold as he turned away from Amon. "It's too late, Amon. The gods abandoned us, left us to suffer while they thrived. I'm done fighting for them. This is the only way."

Shakhti's eyes gleamed with triumph as he watched the scene unfold. He could feel the power within his grasp, the culmination of centuries of planning and destruction. "Venan," Shakhti said, his voice a low, menacing growl, "your brother is right. Surrender your power to me, and I will spare you. You have my word."

Venan's mind raced, his thoughts a whirlwind of anger, fear, and despair. He couldn't betray everything he believed in, but the thought of facing Shakhti alone, especially with Beren now on his side, was overwhelming. He glanced at Amon, who was barely holding on, and his resolve wavered.

Seeing the hesitation in his brother's eyes, Beren stepped closer, his voice softer, almost pleading. "Venan, please. We've lost too much already. Don't make this harder than it has to be."

Amon, sensing the gravity of the moment, summoned what little strength he had left. "Venan, listen to me," he said, his voice filled with urgency. "Shakhti is a monster, and if you give him your power, he will destroy everything. You are stronger than this. Don't let him win."

Venan's eyes flickered with uncertainty, but Beren's influence was strong. Torn between his loyalty to his brother and his duty to stop their father, he felt himself slipping. The weight of the decision was crushing, and the dark world around them seemed to close in, suffocating him.

Finally, with a deep breath, Venan made his choice. "I... I can't fight you both," he whispered, his voice barely audible. "I'm sorry."

With that, Venan extended his hand, the flames that had once burned so brightly now dimming as he prepared to surrender his power to Shakhti. A dark, swirling vortex of energy began to form between them, drawing in Venan's strength, his very essence, as Shakhti's power grew even more.

Amon's heart sank as he watched the scene unfold. He knew what was coming, but he was powerless to stop it. His own strength was nearly gone; his divine energy drained from the relentless assault. As he struggled to move, to intervene, he could feel the darkness closing in around him.

Shakhti's laughter echoed through the dark world as he absorbed Venan's power, the energy coursing through him like a raging storm. "Yes," Shakhti hissed, his voice filled with malevolent glee, "give me your power, and I will reshape the universe in my image. None will stand against me!"

But as the transfer of power continued, Venan suddenly felt a surge of regret. His thoughts were filled with memories of the battles he had fought, the lives he had saved, and the promises he had made. He couldn't let it end like this. He couldn't betray everything he had ever fought for.

In a final, desperate act, Venan summoned the last of his strength, pulling back from the vortex. "No!" he shouted; his voice filled with determination. "I won't do it! I won't let you win!"

But the act of pulling away had already weakened him, and Shakhti's grip was too strong. The dark energy continued to drain him, even as he tried to resist. Beren, watching his brother's struggle, hesitated for a moment, a flicker of doubt crossing his face.

And then, in a flash of divine light, Amon made his move. Summoning the last of his divine energy, he launched himself at Shakhti, his body glowing with a blinding brilliance. The impact was like a star exploding, the force of it shaking the very foundations of the dark world.

Shakhti staggered, caught off guard by the sudden assault. But Amon's strength was nearly spent, and Shakhti quickly regained his composure. With a snarl of rage, he lashed out, his dark energy engulfing Amon and pulling him into the vortex.

"No!" Venan screamed, watching in horror as Amon was consumed by the darkness. He tried to move, to fight, but his strength was gone, his power drained.

Shakhti's eyes burned with fury as he held Amon in his grasp. "You've interfered for the last time, Amon. Now, you will die."

Amon's gaze met Venan's one last time, a sad, knowing look in his eyes. "Venan... run," he whispered, his voice barely audible over the roaring energy.

And then, with a final surge of dark power, Shakhti unleashed his supreme attack. The vortex of energy exploded, engulfing Amon in a storm of destruction. The light that had once radiated from Amon flickered and dimmed, and then, in an instant, it was gone.

Venan watched in stunned silence as the light of Amon's life was snuffed out, the divine energy dissipating into the void. A deep, crushing sorrow filled his heart as he realized what had just happened. Amon, the god who had fought to protect them, who had tried to save them all, was dead.

Shakhti's laughter echoed through the dark world, a sound of pure, malevolent triumph. "He's gone," Shakhti said, his voice filled with satisfaction. "And now, there's nothing left to stop me."

But even in his grief, Venan knew he couldn't stay. Amon's last words echoed in his mind: *Run.*

With the last of his strength, Venan turned and fled, his heart heavy with the weight of his failure. The dark world around him seemed to close in, the shadows whispering threats and curses as he stumbled through the desolate landscape. But he kept moving, driven by the desperate need to escape, to survive.

Behind him, Shakhti's voice called out, mocking and cruel. "Run, Venan! Run and hide! But know this: there is no place in this universe where you can escape me. I will find you, and when I do, you will wish you had died with Amon!"

But Venan didn't stop. He couldn't stop. The memory of Amon's sacrifice drove him forward, the knowledge that he had to live, to fight another day. He had to find a way to stop Shakhti, to prevent the destruction of everything Amon had died to protect.

With every step, Venan felt the weight of his brother's betrayal, the loss of his mentor, and the crushing realization that he was now truly alone. But he also felt a spark of determination, a flicker of hope that refused to be extinguished.

As he ran, the dark world around him began to fade, the oppressive shadows giving way to a dim light in the distance. Venan pushed himself harder, his body aching, his mind racing. He didn't know where he was going, but he knew he had to keep moving.

Finally, after what felt like an eternity, Venan burst through the darkness and into the light. He found himself standing on the edge of a vast, desolate plain, the sky above him filled with swirling clouds of dark energy. But he was free, for now.

Gasping for breath, Venan collapsed to the ground, his body trembling with exhaustion and grief. He had lost everything—his brother, his mentor, and his hope. But he was still alive, and as long as he lived, there was a chance to fight back.

A chance to avenge Amon's death and stop Shakhti before it was too late.

With a heavy heart, Venan pushed himself to his feet, his mind already beginning to form a plan. He had to find allies, to gather what strength he could. Shakhti was more powerful than ever, but Venan wasn't going to give up.

He would find a way to stop his father, even if it cost him everything.

And as he walked away from the dark world, leaving behind the echoes of his past, Venan made a silent vow: *I will not let your sacrifice be in vain, Amon. I will stop him, no matter the cost.*

The death of Amon shattered the fragile balance holding the cosmos together. His absence carved a void so vast it pulsed across dimensions, unravelling reality itself. Earth trembled, convulsing in waves of seismic terror; fault lines split open like gaping maws, swallowing entire cities without warning. Tsunami sirens wailed across continents, a discordant chorus to nature's rising fury.

The skies grew feverish, thick with the scent of scorched ozone. A solar tempest brewed ominously at the sun's surface, its magnetic breath lashing toward Earth with chaotic precision. Heat surged unnaturally, as if the planet were being drawn into the heart of a dying star. Gravity wavered—unsure, inconsistent—as laws of physics buckled beneath the strain. Time felt slower. Angles bent wrongly. Light faltered. Then the moon began its ominous descent.

Looming larger each night, it crept across the heavens with unsettling proximity, its surface eerily illuminated like an unwelcome witness. Tides rebelled. Minds fractured. As cosmic order collapsed, the universe mourned its lost god not with silence—but with unrelenting, cataclysmic fury.

Amon was gone. And reality was remembering him in screams. People in Mumbai were about to witness an unnatural boil in Arabian sea and a figure emerging from the depth of ocean in upcoming days. Shakhti thought he had defeated gods by killing Amoon but he was unaware of what he was about to face soon.

TO BE CONTINUED...

SHAKHTI

First Omens of Ragnarök

Story creates an initial foundation for the long go.

AMON

The Last Hope

Story of Amon being a part of Gods fighting battles against demon supreme. His journey from antient times million years ago is narrated in the story.

VENAN

Brotherhood

Mystery of Venan and Beren ending up with the rage against SHAKHTI.

RAGNARÖK

The Era of Darkness

The great war among Gods and Demons in present time.

Author's Note:

Thank you for reading *Shakhti.* Crafting this story has been an incredible journey, filled with both challenges and excitement. The inspiration for *Shakhti* came from a fascination with the interplay of myth, power, and the human psyche. The world of demons, gods, and supernatural forces allowed me to explore themes of identity, conflict, and redemption in a setting that is as thrilling as it is otherworldly.I want to extend my deepest gratitude to the many people who helped bring this story to life. To my editor, whose keen insights and unwavering support shaped the narrative, and to my beta readers, whose enthusiasm and feedback were invaluable, thank you. Your contributions have been instrumental in refining the story and ensuring its impact. A special thank you goes to the readers who have embraced the world of *Shakhti.* Your support means everything to me, and I hope this book has provided you with the same thrill and wonder that fueled its creation. As with all stories of the supernatural, *Shakhti* is a tapestry of imagination and reality. It draws on ancient myths and modern thrills, blending them into a narrative that I hope will leave you questioning the boundaries of our world and the powers that lie beyond. For those who are eager for more, stay tuned. The story of Shakhti is far from over, and there are many more secrets waiting to be uncovered.

Thank you for joining me on this journey. I look forward to sharing more stories with you in the future.

Warmest regards,

SHREYAS KOSHTI

www.ingramcontent.com/pod-product-compliance
Lightning Source LLC
Chambersburg PA
CBHW050015170726
48282CB00025B/407
* 9 7 8 9 3 3 4 3 5 3 6 0 0 *